She thought she heard a sound. Sarah lifted her head, and through a mist of tears and eyelash rainbows she saw Shadow, about a hundred yards away, sitting and facing her. As soon as she saw the cat, it stood, turned, and walked around one of the blind corners in the trail.

"I'm cracking up," Sarah said. "It's really true. I'm gonna have to tell my parents and they'll put me in some Shady Glen or something until I'm better." She felt almost good now that everything was so bizarre. "Maybe I'm not even lost in the woods!" she continued as if she had an invisible audience. "I'm probably home watching TV!" In this spirit of absurdity she felt much better. She got up and walked in the direction she thought the cat had gone, and sure enough, when she rounded the corner, there was Shadow again, sitting and waiting. Sarah began to walk toward the cat slowly, hoping it would stay and let her catch up. It occurred to her that maybe she wasn't completely hallucinating. There could, after all, be a black cat in the woods. Not Shadow but some black cat looking for shrews and mice. At least following it gave her something constructive to do instead of crying her eyes out and picturing herself in an institution.

JOYCE SWEENEY's first book, *Center Line*, won the First Annual Delacorte Press Prize for an Outstanding First Young Adult Novel. She has also written *The Tiger Orchard, Face the Dragon, The Dream Collector, Right Behind the Rain,* and *Piano Man.* She works as a freelance book critic and is a board member of the Book Group of South Florida. She lives in Coral Springs, Florida, with her husband, Jay, and cat, Macoco.

Shadow

Joyce Sweeney

LAUREL·LEAF BOOKS

Published by
Dell Publishing
a division of
Bantam Doubleday Dell Publishing Group, Inc.
1540 Broadway
New York, New York 10036

ISBN: 0-440-21986-8

RL: 6.2

Reprinted by arrangement with Delacorte Press

Printed in the United States of America

May 1996

10 9 8 7 6 5 4 3 2 1

OPM

To the Traveling Tea Ladies of
Greater Fort Lauderdale;
Victoria Reichmann, Joan Mazza,
and Heidi Boehringer,
with deep appreciation
for their help and support

One

Sarah waited for the class to settle down, listening for the Quiet. Quiet was essential to good writing; as important as clean, blank paper. That was why Sarah did most of her real work at school or in the library. Never at home.

Every Friday afternoon the Nova School had creative writing for the eighth grade. That was how Sarah discovered she was really a writer. She'd suspected it anyway, because her mom was a writer. Sarah had grown up reading books and newspapers, scribbling little poems the family made a fuss over. But it was only when she began to compete with kids her own age that Sarah knew she was special.

It was catalyst writing this afternoon. Ms. Devon had propped up a black-and-white photo of a little boy, a black kid about ten years old, gazing through a chain-link fence. They were supposed to make up a story about him. Sarah already knew what the other kids in the class would write. For confirmation she glanced over at her best friend, Julian Lopez, who was laboring in his slow, careful hand:

> *Jordan stared through the chain-link fence at the basketball court, where the big guys were playing. I wish I was tall, he thought.*

That, Sarah knew, was the trouble with most people's writing. They took the first idea that popped into their heads. Sarah's mother had told her once, "Garbage floats on the surface." There was nothing wrong with a story about a short kid who wanted to play basketball, but Sarah knew that somewhere in the Quiet, if she kept listening, she'd hear a better story.

The room was very still now, nothing but the soft scuffing of hands dragging across pages. Sarah uncapped her hot-pink felt-tip pen—a gift from her brother Patrick—and began:

> *Trash blew across the prison yard. Cigarette butts, crumpled legal sheets, silver bits of candy-paper that flashed in the sun. Corey rested his forehead against the fence and closed his eyes, trying to picture his mother in this horrible place where he wasn't even allowed to visit her. He imagined her like convicts he'd seen on TV, sitting on a cot suspended from chains, wearing a dull blue dress that looked wrong with her skin. He wondered if she thought about him a lot.*

"You must be some kind of genius," Julian said as they walked home together. They only lived a few houses apart.

Ms. Devon had collected the papers at the end of the period and read the best ones out loud. One of the best ones, as usual, was "Prison Yard Blues" by Sarah Isabel Jane Shaheen.

"It's nothing." Sarah shrugged. "It's like you and science."

Julian read physics books for fun. He had a poster of Stephen Hawking in his room. Sarah had Stephen King.

"Are you doing anything this weekend?" Julian asked her. "I want to see *One Hundred and One Dalmatians.*"

Sarah smiled. That was why she liked Julian so much. No, actually there were a million reasons. She liked his shyness and seriousness, his gentle brown eyes framed by horn-rims, the slow, careful way he worked with his hands . . . but mostly she liked him because he was an individual. Any other guy in her class would be heading for some blood-and-vengeance movie this weekend. Julian wanted to see *101 Dalmatians.*

"I can't this weekend," Sarah said. "Remember? Classes just ended at UF. My brother Brian is coming home for the summer. So the Asylum will be in an uproar."

Julian made a face. "Watching Brian come home takes the whole weekend?"

"Sure. Tonight Mom will go nuts trying to clean the house with no maid. Tomorrow we meet his plane. Then we have to take him out to dinner—no maid again—and all day Sunday I'll have to referee family fights."

He chuckled. "Sneak out to the movies with me Sunday. Let them fight."

"Well . . ." Sarah always hesitated before accepting invitations so that Julian would never suspect how crazy she was about him. She understood fourteen-year-old boys very well. "But I have to keep Brian from killing Patrick."

Julian shoved his hands in his pockets, pouting. "Patrick's a big boy. He can take care of himself."

"You're half right," Sarah said. They were in front of her house now, so they stopped walking and faced each other. "I'll call you, okay?"

He hesitated, then turned away. "Okay." He slouched off, head down.

Sarah watched, smiling, until he was out of sight. The breeze blew a long, curling strand of hair into her face. Before she tossed it back, Sarah held it up to the sun, admiring its bright golden color. She was the only bionde in the family. She gave her books a little hug and went into the house.

Her mother was sitting across the dining room table from a new prospective maid. She'd been interviewing all week. The Shaheens had run through about twenty maids in the last five years. They'd had a thief, a political radical who made phone calls all day, a refrigerator raider, a soap-opera addict, a religious fanatic, and other assorted characters. The last one had done her work well, but Sarah's mother had caught Sarah's father looking at her too much. That woman left in such a rage, she did something to the upstairs toilet that caused it to explode the first time it was flushed. So now Mrs. Shaheen was being extremely careful in the interview process.

Judy Shaheen was a columnist for the *Fort Lauderdale Sun-Sentinel*. She wrote about real-life situations, which meant she often humiliated her children in print by telling their "amusing" secrets to the whole town. Patrick, for instance, was still being teased in school about a column ten years ago that exposed his morbid fear of storm drains. Mrs. Shaheen was a tall, broad-shouldered woman with dark, swept-back hair and sharp, intelligent features. In any crowd she was always the first person you noticed, or if you didn't, she'd see to it that you did.

Sarah could see from her mother's expression she didn't know what to make of the maid candidate. But the woman didn't seem to notice. She was chattering away in a lilty southern accent, trying to hook a lock of limp hair behind her ear. She was small, pale, and freckled. No trace of makeup. She wore a lavender cardigan that appeared to be swallowing her. More than anything she looked like a little girl posing as an adult.

"And then I worked for Mr. and Mrs. Andrew Loveage of Baton Rouge [she pronounced it *Roudge*], Louisiana. They didn't have any children but Mrs. Loveage was very house-proud and had a real [*rill*] high standard. That's the thing, Mrs. Shaheen [*Sheen*]. All I need to know is what are your standards and then I can live up to them. Everybody's got their little things, like they can't stand fingerprints or dust . . . or they just want the housekeeper to stay away from them and be quiet. Since you work at home a lot, I can appreciate you'd like quiet maybe around the house. I'm a rill good cook and I'm rill good with children and you just tell me what it is you want and that's what I'll do because it's my job to make the house the way you'd make it if you had the time." She paused to crack her gum.

Mrs. Shaheen stared at her a moment, blinking. "Cissy," she said, "this is my daughter, Sarah."

Cissy swiveled as if she'd been offered chocolate

cake. She stuck out a small hand half obscured by sweater cuff. "Hi, Sarah. It sure is nice to meet you. I'm Cissy Champion. I'm interviewing with your mama to be the new maid." She turned back to Mrs. Shaheen. "How many children are there in all?"

Mrs. Shaheen smiled a little. " 'In all' there are three. Sarah is the youngest. She's in the eighth grade. Patrick —you met Patrick briefly—is seventeen. Our oldest son, Brian, is a freshman at the University of Florida. He's taking premed."

"Oh, what an interesting family!" Cissy swiveled back to Sarah. "Your mama told me what an interesting family this is. I mean, your daddy a doctor and your mama a writer. And you kids being so smart and going to special schools. It's just like a TV show."

Mrs. Shaheen smiled again. "I wasn't aware there were any TV shows about intelligent people," she said.

Cissy blinked. "What about *L.A. Law?*"

Sarah decided that was a good time to leave. "I'm going outside," she said.

Mrs. Shaheen opened her mouth as if to object, then appeared to change her mind. Obviously she didn't want to go into the entire Shadow controversy in front of a stranger.

Every day after school Sarah tried to spend some time at Shadow's grave. It wasn't quite a year since the day they took her to the vet for the last time.

Mrs. Shaheen disapproved of the grave, since technically there wasn't anything there. It was against the law to bury cats in Coral Springs. But Sarah had been so stricken by the idea the vet would just take Shadow away and "dispose" of her, she couldn't speak or even think clearly for days.

Patrick had come up with the idea. Sarah could still remember him, skinny and shirtless in the Florida sun, killing himself trying to drive a shovel into the gravelly soil until he and Sarah felt he'd reached the proper depth. Every few minutes Mrs. Shaheen had appeared at the patio door and called out, "If you hit a sprinkler line, young man, you are going to be very, very sorry!"

Ignoring her, he had silently finished his work, gone in the house, showered, and changed into a shirt and tie and put on a blue blazer for the "funeral."

Sarah had buried Shadow's favorite things; a well-chewed crocheted ball, a purple rabbit's foot, a stuffed raccoon. Then she read a poem she had written herself. Patrick took up his shovel again and filled in the hole. (Now the chant from the patio was, "If you get dirt on your good clothes . . .") Sarah put a water glass full of marigolds on the grave, and they had a moment of silence.

"Better?" Patrick had asked as they walked back to the house.

For the first time in days Sarah felt the tightness in her chest ease. "Better," she'd said.

She'd made a promise to herself that day never to forget. Someday Patrick would need something and she'd repay him.

Sarah walked out to the grave now and sat in the grass waiting for the same kind of Quiet she used for writing. It was good for other things as well, for feelings and thoughts and important ideas. Every day when she came here, she got the sensation of time slowing down, maybe even stopping. The only thing she could compare it to was the memory of being a very small child, when she could still "feel" the world around her without a steady stream of thoughts analyzing everything.

The grave was under the hibiscus hedge, where Shadow liked to sleep in the afternoons. Sarah could picture her there now, rolling in the dirt, whipping her tail as she stalked lizards.

The Quiet began to steal over Sarah, stilling her thoughts. *This is how animals think*, she realized. *Just feelings with no words*. The sun, sparkling on the hibiscus leaves, blurred her vision slightly. The wind picked up, gently lifting her hair. The neighborhood sounds began to harmonize into one pulsing rhythm. It seemed to Sarah that the colors around her were dimming, things were blurring together, yet she was keenly aware of motion and a strange shininess, as if everything were alive with its own jumping, dancing energy. She noticed a sharp combination of smells: spiciness from the hibiscus, chlorophyll from the sun-heated grass, a meaty-metallic smell—insects!

Sarah felt as if Shadow was there and right at that moment was showing her the world the way a cat perceives it.

Something seemed to tumble in her mind and Sarah saw herself as a little girl of seven going with her father to the farm in Ocala to get her special birthday present —a real kitten.

She saw the shadowy barn, the cardboard box with tomatoes printed on it, the frayed yellow towel streaked with grease. The mother cat, black and white, preening. And the flailing, squirming kittens.

Shadow had looked up at Sarah. The only kitten who was solid black, with no white markings anywhere. Her eyes were a vivid turquoise that later resolved into jade.

Shadow had stared at Sarah as if she knew her. She left her struggling mass of brothers and sisters and clambered over the edge of the box. She looked into Sarah's eyes and squeaked urgently.

"Do you want to be my kitty?" Sarah had asked, enchanted. She knew nothing about animals. It had been a battle to get her mother to allow this.

The other kittens scrambled and played. Shadow stood quiet and still, looking up at Sarah.

"Can I pick her up?" Sarah said to the lady who owned the farm. She didn't know how she knew Shadow was female.

"Sure thing," said the lady.

Shadow was very small and light. Under the fur her bones felt delicate, like a bird's. She cuddled into Sarah's chest and closed her eyes. Sarah lowered her head and sniffed the Kitten Smell—warm blankets, Cream of Wheat.

"Okay," Sarah said to her father.

He smiled. "Don't you want to even see the other kittens?"

Sarah had held Shadow tighter. "Uh-uh. This is my kitty."

Her ears picked up a rustling in the grass behind her. Cold, fearful excitement fizzed in her blood. She whirled. "Shadow?" she said out loud.

Then she felt like a complete fool. It was Patrick, loping out to her in his clumsy-graceful way. Sarah blushed, hoping he hadn't heard her. Her mother told her she had a dangerous imagination.

He either hadn't heard or was being polite about it. He dropped onto the grass beside her, tossing his fine hair out of his eyes, locking his fingers around his knees. "Hello, little girl," he said. "Is this a private wake or can anybody attend?"

"You can."

"Thank you. I'm honored and flattered. Want to hear the big news?"

"Sure."

"We have a new maid."

"You're kidding. She hired the one that was in the dining room?"

"That's the one. Miss Grits-and-Gravy. Where's she from, anyway? Arkansas?"

"Baton Roudge. Her pronunciation."

"Uh-oh! Voodoo! I think Mom likes her because she calls her ma'am. She'd probably like it if we did that too."

"Fat chance. So when does she start?"

"Tomorrow. She has to create this big feast we're having for the return of Dracula."

Sarah giggled. "Are you going to the airport?"

Patrick looked at her. His eyes were an odd color, a blue so pale, they appeared gray. With his floppy hair he had the look of a weird, soulful dog. "Well, I told Dad I absolutely refused to go. He offered me some options. I decided I wanted to go after all. Karen's coming for dinner tomorrow too." Karen was Brian's girlfriend.

"Oh, great," Sarah said. "We can watch them slobber on each other."

"Ugh. Don't remind me. Listen, kid. I don't want to make you mad, but there's a feeling around the house that you should start to cut back on this graveside-vigil thing. I mean, don't you think Shadow wants to move on and go to cat heaven? You need to get closure and all that good stuff."

"You need to mind your own business and cut the bull. This is obviously Mom talking. Did she send you out here?"

He hung his head. "I thought I was being subtle."

"You're not ever subtle, Trick. You're lots and lots of things, but never subtle."

"Well, just this one time, I happen to agree with Mom. I think it's morbid for you to keep coming out here every day. She's been dead since last summer. If you got another cat—"

"That's Dad talking!"

"Everybody wants to help you, Pixie. This isn't good!"

Sarah hugged her knees. "It makes me feel better. I think she comes out here sometimes to be with me."

"Oh, sweetie, no!"

"It's not crazy. That's not crazy. Millions of people believe in life after death."

"Not for kittycats."

"Buddhists and Hinduists do!"

"Well, you're a lapsed Catholic, so forget it. All we believe in is parental guilt."

"Ha-ha. The trouble with you is that you're too chickenshit to believe in anything."

Patrick stopped smiling and turned away. "Maybe so," he said quietly.

Sarah was surprised. She hadn't meant to make him feel vulnerable. But since she had, she decided to get some value out of it. "Trick?"

He looked at her. "What?"

"Tell me what you really believe. Do you think when we die, that's it?"

He hugged himself. "No."

"Really?"

"Yes. Really."

"Why?"

He frowned. "Well, because the world is so . . . weird. Have you noticed? I mean, why would death be the only thing that actually is what it appears to be?"

Sarah had to play that over several times in her head. "Wow," she said finally.

Patrick got up quickly, brushing off imaginary dirt. "See why I'm never serious? When I am, I come off an even bigger flake than you! Listen, come in the house pretty soon so Mom won't yell at me. Okay?"

"Okay. Just one more minute."

He ruffled her hair and loped back toward the house.

Sarah leaned close to the grave and whispered, "He's one of us."

TWO

Sarah thought it was amazing her father would buy a plane ticket for Brian when he was only coming from Gainesville and had a perfectly good car of his own. But Brian said he didn't like to drive on I-95, and Dr. Shaheen had given in easily, realizing he would have extra time with Brian this way. He hadn't been the same since his firstborn went off to college.

Sarah amused herself in the airport by eavesdropping on other people's conversations. Right behind her, for instance, was a young couple, probably not more than Brian's age. The boy was getting on the plane and he was dumping the girl, but she was too dumb to know it.

"So will you call when you get in?"

"Not right away. I won't have a place. But when I get organized—"

"You'll what? Check into a motel?"

"Yeah, probably."

"You could call me from a motel."

A pause. "Yeah, I'll probably do that."

Not, Sarah thought.

"And how soon will you send for me?"

Kissing noises. Sarah was surprised. It seemed like a funny place in the conversation for that.

"I love you," the girl said drowsily.

"Me, too, baby."

Answer her question! Sarah thought. *Why is this girl so stupid? Can't she hear the insincerity in his voice?*

Some kind of shifting around. Sarah wished she could turn around and watch them, but her mother would probably notice and say something to her. Sarah's mother never missed anything.

"Like, before the month is out? Will you want me to come out before the month is out?"

"It depends on if I get a job. We *talked* about this, babe."

"Will you miss me?"

He laughed a dirty laugh.

Sarah wondered if the girl was pregnant. She stopped listening at this point and began to put in her own details. The girl went from the airport back to her squalid apartment. For a long time she waited for the guy to call. She kept packing her things and making plans. She was pregnant and got huge. She went around in her bathrobe (Sarah saw a battered pink terry cloth, with maybe a bunny stitched on the pocket) and lived on cereal. She began trying to trace the guy, to find a number. She went into labor. She had her baby all alone. . . . Sarah paused. Should it be a sad ending, or should the girl finally learn from all this to stand on her own two feet? Before she could decide, they announced Brian's plane.

Dr. Shaheen bounced up out of his seat like a dog hearing his master's car. Mrs. Shaheen took out her mirrored lipstick case and freshened up. Patrick wasn't with them. He was in the gate next door, looking out the window.

Brian was the first one off the plane. Sarah could picture him jumping up in the aisle before the seatbelt light was off, pulling his carry-on bag off the overhead rack (probably hitting somebody in the head), and charging down the aisle to be the first one at the door.

He was wearing 501s and what looked like a brand-new black leather bike jacket. He was sweating like crazy, but obviously preferred looking good to avoiding heatstroke.

There was a strong resemblance between Patrick and Brian, although neither of them liked to admit it. Brian was a little taller and bigger and wore his hair trimmed short instead of flopping down in his eyes. And their movements and gestures were very different. Patrick had a coltish grace, while Brian charged through life like a bull.

He plowed toward his family now with such force, it made other people jump out of his way. He went straight to his father, bear-hugging him.

"How *are* you?" Dr. Shaheen cried, although they'd just spoken on the telephone that morning. "God! The house seems so empty without you."

"It's very peaceful and quiet," Mrs. Shaheen quipped, breaking up the hug and pulling Brian into her own arms. She patted him fondly, *one, two, three, your time is up*, and released him. "For heaven's sake, take off that jacket," she told him. "You'll smother. Incidentally is that new?"

He flushed. "Yeah. I . . . Pixie!" He embraced Sarah, obviously to create a diversion. The smell of sweaty leather was overwhelming. Then he stood up again, looking around, smirking. "Where's Patricia?"

Mrs. Shaheen folded her arms. "Don't you dare start that stuff up with your brother again! You're a grown man now. It wasn't cute when you were a little boy and it's definitely not cute now! If you can't control yourself, you can stay in a motel for the summer!"

Brian had been making gender jokes about Patrick since they were kids, but in the last few years Mrs. Shaheen had gotten more upset about it. Sarah thought this was possibly because her mother believed there was some truth to it. Sarah herself didn't know or care what Patrick was into. She knew she would love him the same either way, and if he wanted to tell her about it, he could.

"It's just a joke," Brian said.

Mrs. Shaheen narrowed her eyes. "It's not funny."

There was an edgy silence.

"Let's all try to get along, at least until we get into the parking lot," Dr. Shaheen pleaded. "Patrick! Brian's here!"

"I see him," Patrick called over his shoulder.

Dr. Shaheen went over to Patrick and spoke quietly to him. Patrick followed him back, dragging his feet. "Hello," he muttered to Brian.

"Hello." Brian turned away from him, addressing the others. "Is Karen coming tonight?"

"Yes," said Mrs. Shaheen. "We're having a special dinner for you. We have a new cook and she's making Cajun food."

"Creole," said Sarah.

"Pardon?" Mrs. Shaheen looked down at her.

"Creole is different from Cajun. Cissy explained it to me. Creole is—"

"She's making food from Louisiana," Mrs. Shaheen said to Brian.

"I don't know if I can eat that stuff," he warned. The Florida heat finally overcame him, and he shucked his jacket, revealing a soaked T-shirt.

"It must be spring," Patrick said. "The snakes are shedding their skins."

"It must be spring!" Brian mimicked. "The fairies are coming out of the woods!"

Mrs. Shaheen turned wearily to Sarah. "Sit between them in the car," she said.

Sarah answered the door. It was Karen in a silk dress and high heels. Her eyelashes were matted with mascara and her lids were lavender all the way to the eyebrows. Karen had been instrumental in Sarah's decision never to wear makeup.

Karen was seventeen, a year behind Brian in school. Last fall, when he went away to college, she'd acted like she was having a nervous breakdown. She still came over and hung around the house, kissing up to Mrs. Shaheen and trying to determine if various family members thought Brian was being faithful to her. Once, she'd even asked Sarah to help her write a romantic letter to Brian, but when Sarah found out what *romantic* really meant, she resigned from the project.

"Hello, honey!" Karen said. She always spoke to Sarah as if she were a small child. Karen peered into the house like Alice in Wonderland looking through the keyhole into the beautiful garden. "Is he here?" She giggled.

Sarah escorted her into the living room, where Brian was sprawled on the couch, drinking beer from the can. Dr. Shaheen sat close by, watching Brian's every move as if he were a glorious kaleidoscope.

"Oh, Brian!" Karen squeaked from the doorway.

He looked up. "Hey, babe."

Sarah sighed. Just like the guy in the airport. Someday she would write a handbook for women. The title would be, *If He Calls You Babe, Watch Out!*

Brian sat up and put his beer can on the glass-topped coffee table. He winked at his father and then said to Karen in his best sexy voice. "Come here."

Sarah watched with mild disgust as Karen walked forward like a sheep about to be sheared. Brian grabbed her wrists and pulled her down on the couch beside him. Her skirt flew up. Dr. Shaheen smiled absently. Brian put some kind of wrestling hold on Karen and subjected her to a violent-looking kiss while she squirmed, trying to get loose and pull her dress down at the same time.

Sarah decided not to look at her father. She was trying to hang onto the idea that he could still be her hero for a few more years, but he made it difficult sometimes. Since she didn't want to look at Karen and Brian, she concentrated on the Coors can, watching streams of condensation pool on the glass tabletop. Now it would have to be cleaned with Windex. There were coasters all over the room, but Brian always ignored them.

Karen finally struggled free and sat up next to Brian, tugging her skirt over her knees. Both the men were laughing, and Karen was laughing, too, but it was a short, barking laugh, like a child who's been tickled beyond endurance.

"Did you miss me?" Brian giggled.

"You're bad." Karen smiled. "Very, very bad."

Sarah decided to leave before she got sick.

Against her better judgment she went down the hall to Patrick's room. He had been sulking there all afternoon. Sarah loved Patrick more than anyone in the world, but when he was feeling sorry for himself, he was pretty revolting. Still, no one else in the family was going to bother with him, so Sarah had to.

When Brian was still at home, he shared this room with Patrick. It had been a schizophrenic place in those days. An invisible line ran between the twin beds. On Patrick's side, the far side, everything was neat and clean. The far wall was decorated with movie posters and lobby cards; *Some Like It Hot, Breakfast at Tiffany's, Desire Under the Elms*. On Patrick's dresser there was a framed reproduction of Andy Warhol's Marilyn Monroe. Patrick was obsessed with Marilyn Monroe. His bookshelf was crammed with biographies of her. If you let him, he would talk for hours about the conspiracy theories. Sarah had learned never to bring the topic up.

On Brian's side of the room, in the old days, there had been piles of underwear and smelly socks and skin magazines. Brian's walls had NFL posters, *Playboy* centerfolds, and pictures of Corvettes, all unframed and taped up crookedly. His dresser top always held objects you didn't really want to see—condoms, used Kleenex, athletic supporters.

Since Brian went away to school, the cleanliness and order had spread across the whole room. Over Brian's bed, where there was once a picture of a girl straddling a beach ball, there was now James Dean, looking like he was about to have a nervous breakdown.

Now, as Sarah walked in, Patrick was sitting on his bed, hugging his knees, staring grimly at the pile of luggage near Brian's bed as if he thought any minute it would explode and litter the room with all of Brian's former junk.

"Aren't you coming out to join the party?" Sarah asked.

Patrick sighed theatrically. "Why can't he die?" he asked.

"Hey!" Sarah said. "Don't. That's not even a good joke, and you don't really mean it." She sat down on Brian's bed.

Patrick seemed to speak to Brian's luggage instead of to Sarah. "How come he couldn't bring his damn car? Huh? Now he's going to want to use my car, and Dad will let him. It's like I don't even exist."

Sarah resisted the urge to tell him how childlike his voice had become as he said this. Even the pitch was higher than normal. "It was Brian's car before he handed it down to you. So I guess he has some rights, doesn't he?"

Patrick pulled his knees up tighter. "You think Dad will ever buy me a new car? No. I'll be driving Brian's hand-me-downs forever."

Sarah was fed up. "Not necessarily. Maybe someday you'll grow up. Then you can buy yourself a new car."

He laughed. "I know how I sound," he admitted. "I can't help it. I get around him and I just get so mad. . . ."

Sarah lowered her eyes. "It's because of the way he teases you. The jokes he makes."

Patrick didn't answer.

Sarah looked up at him. "You have to learn how to ignore him."

Apparently he wasn't in the mood for advice. "Who was at the door? The bimbo?"

Sarah decided to cut this visit short. "If you mean Karen, yes. Why don't you come out and say hi to her?"

"Oh, right!"

"Or let's go in the kitchen and see what Cissy's cooking. It smells great, doesn't it?"

"Sarah, thanks for the effort, but I'm really sort of into my self-pity right now."

"Well, everybody should have a hobby," she said, sliding off the bed.

He hung his head. "I'm sorry."

He was such a jerk. Sarah went to him and gave him a hug. She didn't know what she would do when he grew up and went away.

"Jesus!" he muttered, but he didn't resist.

Out in the hall the kitchen smells were overwhelming. Sarah went to investigate.

Cissy was now dressed in a fascinating pale pink blouse with a floppy flounce at the neck. A small silver heart dangled from her wrist. She was hopping around the kitchen like a sparrow, looking in the cupboards, stirring mysterious pots on the stove, scanning the refrigerator with a serious, squinty expression. "We gotta make a shopping list," she said to Mrs. Shaheen, who was perched on a stool, sipping vermouth.

"Okay," said Mrs. Shaheen. "Go on with your story. How soon did your parents know about you?"

"Well, I wasn't born with a caul or anything like that. You know what that is?"

Mrs. Shaheen nodded, sipping. Sarah realized she had never seen her mother listening so attentively to anyone before.

"And I wasn't a twin or anything—no cayenne? I'll just have to try with black pepper—but I did have green eyes. So my grandmama said I might have it. She said green eyes were a marker for second sight."

"And you actually worked for the police department?"

"Yeah. But I had to quit. It was too depressing. Seeing all those . . . regular people don't realize, Mrs. Shaheen"—she still pronounced it *Sheen*—"the kinds of things the police have to deal with. Murders and . . . it's not like on TV. I was losing my optimism, and I'm a very optimistic person. I pride myself on it. But day after day, when you see what the criminal element is up to, well, you start to lose your optimism. You know?"

Mrs. Shaheen leaned forward. "Are you talking about being at a crime scene? Or seeing these things in your head?"

"Both. Do you have any bitters? Angostura bitters? I don't suppose you do. But this dish is better—"

"We have bitters. Dr. Shaheen insists on having a fully stocked bar. Sarah, run and get them for Cissy. It's a tiny, little bottle."

"What's a caul?" Sarah asked.

"It's like a little sack babies are born in," Cissy answered. "People say it means the baby will be psychic. But I wasn't born that way, I just—"

"Cissy believes she's psychic," Mrs. Shaheen said. "She worked for the New Orleans Police Department as a police psychic."

Sarah edged forward. "How does it work?"

Cissy gave something a stir and fanned steam under her nose, sniffing. "Oh they'd call me up and say, 'There's a woman missing in Meterie.' Then they'd tell me all the details they knew until I felt something. I'd blurt out, 'She's run off,' or 'She's dead.' Then if they wanted to, like, find the body—this is the part I just didn't like—they'd give me something that belonged to the person—a wallet or a string of pearls—and I'd hold it and see . . . where the person was. Mostly it was always the same. In the woods, half naked, rotting away. I hated those visions. So I quit."

"Wow," said Sarah.

"You were making educated guesses," Mrs. Shaheen said. "You don't really believe it was—"

"No, ma'am. I saw those things. I gave the police

exact locations. Oh, sometimes I'd go blank. Like, not see anything at all. But if I did see something, it was accurate. Where's my bitters, honey? You have to time when you put them in, or it ruins the whole dish."

Sarah ran to get them.

Cissy shook a few drops into the biggest pot, counted to ten and stirred. Then she inhaled steam again. "Perfect! We eat in five minutes."

"What are you cooking?" Sarah asked.

"Jambalaya. Shrimp, rice, tomatoes, and anything else I could find. The other pan is okra."

"They smell wonderful," Sarah said.

"Thanks." Cissy turned the burner off. "Timing is everything with this stuff. It has to reduce just enough, not too much. So anyway—I need some serving bowls—anyway, after the police department I tried to use my abilities in a better way. I opened up a fortune-telling business. Tarot cards and all. But that was bad too. My customers all got hooked. They'd come back day after day, checking every little decision. I didn't want to take so much of their money. So I left the Quarter altogether. I moved to Baton Rouge and became a housekeeper and I'm surprised how much I like it." While she spoke, she was shoveling the most colorful, fascinating food Sarah had ever seen into serving bowls.

"Did you ever hold a séance?" Sarah said. "Or talk to spirits?"

"Sure." Cissy finished dishing up the okra and licked her little finger. "Well, not talk to them, but I could see and feel spirits around some of my clients. You could pour the wine now, Mrs. Shaheen. We're ready."

Mrs. Shaheen got up, looking dazed, and walked out.

"Cissy?" Sarah said softly.

Cissy looked at her. In this light her eyes were very green. "What is it?"

"I want to ask you something really important. Do you think dogs and cats have a soul?"

Cissy folded her arms. Her eyes appraised Sarah. "You want to know something about a cat?"

Sarah felt lurchy inside, like when you leave a trampoline and try to walk on solid floors. "Maybe."

"Black cat? Female? She died not too long ago?"

Sarah's thoughts were like whirlpools. One whirlpool was doubt, one was hope, one was terror, one was pure, raw excitement. "Yes," she choked out. "How do you know?"

Cissy shrugged. "You're very easy. Maybe you're a good sender. I can see the cat. Look, why don't you help me with the dishes after dinner and we'll talk about it some more?"

"Okay."

"Don't freak out on me, honey. It seems scary, but it's really no big deal. Here." She shoved the bowl of okra into Sarah's hands. The smell up close was overpowering, something warm and seductive, yams and nutmeg, but a sinister undertone, like seawater. Sarah felt dizzy, but she managed to walk into the dining room, where the family was gathering around the table, drawn by the smells.

"Wow!" said Dr. Shaheen. "This looks great. I feel like we're in a foreign country!"

Not even close, Sarah thought. *We're in a whole different world.*

Three

People were talking all around her, plates were passed, silverware clanked. Sarah's mind was far away, analyzing what Cissy had just said. How could she have done that? How could she have known about Shadow?

Cissy flitted in from the kitchen, checking on everyone, refilling Dad's and Brian's wineglasses, blushing at the tidal wave of compliments to her food. *How could anyone with a face like that be a con artist?* But she had to be.

It was yesterday. When Sarah came home from school, she'd met Cissy and gone straight to Shadow's grave. Of course that was it. Mom had sent Patrick out to get her. The whole thing had probably been discussed in front of Cissy! And now she was using it to pretend she was cosmic! What kind of person would exploit the most sacred, emotional thing in a person's life?

Sarah turned her head and peered through the kitchen doorway. Cissy was sitting on a stool, swinging her feet, looking out the window at mourning doves on the bird feeder. *I'll get her*, Sarah thought.

"You haven't said anything about your grades last semester," Mrs. Shaheen said to Brian.

He looked up, startled, chewing rapidly on the mouthful of rice he'd just shoveled in. "Huh?"

Mrs. Shaheen enunciated carefully. "Your *grades*. A term just ended. You're supposed to come home with a grade printout. Remember? Like that miserable effort you presented to us last winter?"

Brian gulped wine. "I have a printout. I just don't know where it is. I didn't unpack anything yet."

She took a sip of wine. "Well, just tell us what your grades were."

Brian was flushed.

Sarah glanced at Patrick. He was smiling.

"You mean, what my grades were?" Brian asked his mother.

Mrs. Shaheen put her fork down. "Yes, Brian. What your grades for last semester were."

Karen was watching Brian anxiously, the way a bowler watches a ball headed for the gutter.

"Oh," said Brian. He took a biscuit and buttered it violently. "I can't remember."

"Wait until he's settled in, dear," said Dr. Shaheen. "Give him a chance to catch his breath."

"I thought he was doing that all afternoon when you drank the six-pack together," she said. "And I don't think this is such a difficult question. He only takes five classes and there are only five potential grades. . . ."

Brian's face was very red now. "Do we have to discuss it this minute?" He cut his eyes toward Karen. "Can't we talk about it after dinner?"

"Sure," said his father.

"No," said his mother.

Brian turned to his father, pleading with his eyes.

"How bad could it be, son?" Dr. Shaheen asked nervously.

Brian's voice got low. "Pretty bad."

Karen looked down at her plate.

"Well?" Patrick said. "Don't keep us in suspense. Are you flunking out or what?"

Mrs. Shaheen gave him a warning look. "I can handle this myself."

Brian spoke in an old-man's voice. "I'm failing in chemistry and physics. I got a D in English lit., a C in Spanish and a B-plus in music appreciation."

"No problem," Patrick said. "Instead of being a doctor you can become a bilingual disk jockey."

"We don't need your wit at this particular moment!" Dr. Shaheen told him.

Patrick hung his head.

"It's not like I don't try!" Brian stammered. "It's just that some of this stuff is very hard! There's all these . . . formulas and . . . stuff to memorize . . . I worked hard, I really did, it's just that—"

"He's stupid," Patrick said quietly.

Dr. Shaheen whirled on him. "What did I just say?"

"I'm sorry," Patrick muttered.

"Maybe you've been spending a little too much time out shopping for leather jackets and not enough hitting the books," Mrs. Shaheen said to Brian.

Brian kept his eyes on his father. "No, I think it's that . . . Dad, I don't think I'm as good at some of these things as you are. I mean, I know you'd like me to be a doctor and join your practice and all that, but maybe I don't exactly have that kind of talent. If I switched my major—"

"Oh, now let's don't be hasty!" Dr. Shaheen said. "You shouldn't give up so easily. It was hard for me my first year too. Premed is very hard."

"What grades did *you* get?" Brian asked him.

"Well . . . that's beside the point. If you had a tutor, maybe—"

"Dad, I don't like it!" Brian blurted. "I hate science and I hate math! And I wish you wouldn't make me feel like I'm doing something to you personally if I decide not to do the exact same thing with my life that you did!"

Dr. Shaheen looked as if he'd been slapped. "What do you want to do with your life?"

"Obviously he wants to screw it up," Patrick said.

Dr. Shaheen turned to him slowly. "If I hear so much as one more word from you for the rest of this meal, you are going to be one very sorry young man. I mean, I don't want to hear your voice at all. If you so much as ask for the salt—"

"Okay! Okay!"

"If I could get into this conversation," Brian said. "I was thinking of maybe switching to prelaw."

"With a D in English?" Mrs. Shaheen said.

"I could bring that up. I had a real bad class this term. We had to read some kind of crap by André Gide."

He glanced at Patrick. "It would have been right up your alley."

"What does that mean?" Patrick demanded.

Mrs. Shaheen turned to her husband, who appeared to have tears in his eyes. "Maybe he takes more after my side of the family," she said. "You know how bad I am at empirical things."

"Yes," he said softly. "But—"

"I know you're disappointed in me," Brian said. "But I did try, Dad. I really tried."

"We'll discuss it later," Mrs. Shaheen said, watching her husband nervously. He had taken his napkin out of his lap and was holding it up to his face.

There was a long, tense silence. Brian drained off the rest of his wine. He tried to catch his father's eye, but Dr. Shaheen was looking at his plate.

Sarah tried to think of something neutral to say, but all she could think about was what Cissy did to her and how to get revenge.

Karen smiled as stiffly as a Miss America contender. "It's really great to have you home, Bri. Are you doing anything tomorrow? I was thinking maybe we could go on a picnic? Remember that time last summer when—"

Brian shoved food around. "Last summer I was a kid in high school."

Karen inhaled sharply. "Does that mean you don't want to go?"

He shrugged. "It's just . . . I don't know . . . that kind of stuff sounds really juvenile to me now. When you're in college, you just go out like normal adults. You don't have little picnics and shit."

"Brian . . ." Mrs. Shaheen began.

"Picnics and *stuff*," he said.

Karen looked at him, trying to get him to make eye contact but he wouldn't. "So, what? You went off to college and you're a whole different person?"

"Don't worry," Patrick said. "It doesn't sound like he'll be in college much longer anyway."

Dr. Shaheen's fist hit the table so hard, the silverware rattled. "Patrick, what did I say to you?"

Patrick flinched. "Something about keeping my mouth shut?"

"If you forget again, just consider yourself grounded for a couple of weeks. Okay?"

Patrick nodded.

"Answer me out loud!"

"Okay!"

Sarah was beginning to think maybe she would go with Julian to the movies the next day.

Mrs. Shaheen turned to Patrick. "That reminds me. Whatever happened to Melissa?"

Brian snorted a laugh.

Patrick kept his eyes down. "What do you mean what happened to her? She's still alive, as far as I know."

"I mean, why don't you ever take her out?"

"Why should I? You fixed me up with her. I didn't like her."

"Why not?"

" 'Cause she was a girl," Brian said.

"Because she was an idiot!" Patrick flared. "I don't understand why you would think I would want to—"

"It's very important," said Mrs. Shaheen, "for boys your age to socialize."

"Well, fine! But let me do it my own way, all right?"

"Look out, Mom," said Brian. "He might invite the Vienna Boys Choir over for tea."

Patrick stared at him. Then he turned to Dr. Shaheen, who was absently pushing things around on his plate. "How come you won't let me pick on him but you let him say things like that to me?"

"Because he knows this is true!" Brian said.

Patrick stumbled to his feet, knocking his chair over. "I hate this whole family!" he shouted and fled. The door to his room slammed.

Sarah decided she'd been quiet long enough. "He's right, Daddy," she said. "You stick up for Brian, but you don't stick up for him."

"It's a different situation," Dr. Shaheen said. "Brian is just kidding. That's the way guys tease each other. Patrick has to learn not to let it bother him."

"That sounds like justifying," Sarah said.

"That's enough," Mrs. Shaheen told her. "Even though you're absolutely right."

Dr. Shaheen put his fork down with a clatter. "If I step in and help him in a situation like that, it makes him look weak. He has to learn to defend himself."

"That's right," Brian said. "He's nothing but a whining little baby. He wants the whole world to wipe his nose for him." He turned to Karen. "Okay, I guess I can go on this stupid picnic. How do you want to work it?"

Karen stared at him a long time. Then she stood up. She was trembling all over like water about to boil. "Never mind, Brian," she said quietly. "I think if I look around, I can find somebody who wants to go with me and who won't consider it some kind of big favor! Thank

you for dinner, Mrs. Shaheen." She walked out. The
front door slammed.

Brian sighed and reached across the table for Patrick's wine. "This isn't my day," he said.

Cissy washed dishes by candlelight. She said it was
relaxing. "Overhead lights make me jumpy." Sarah felt
this was just showmanship, but she had to admit there
was something comforting about the flickering shadows
on the walls. In this light Cissy lost her washed-out look
and took on a tawny glow. She had already scraped the
plates and loaded the dishwasher, and now she was running a sinkful of soapy water for the crystal. The hot-
water tap was on full, spraying soap bubbles and scenting
the air with artificial violets.

Sarah pulled up a stool and sat down. "You played a
little game with me before, didn't you?"

Cissy held up a goblet and squinted at it. A rainbow
crossed her face. "When?"

"About my cat. You heard about her from my
mother."

Sarah was braced for a fight, but Cissy only laughed.
"No! She didn't speak to me about it."

"Yesterday, after I met you, I went out in back to visit
her grave. You and Mom must have talked about it."

Cissy looked at her. "You've got a cat buried in the
backyard? Isn't that against the law?"

"It's a symbolic grave."

"Oh. Well, I'm sorry to blow your theory, sugar, but
your mama didn't say a word to me about your cat. I

looked at you and saw the cat in my head. That's the best way to explain it. You see, it happens to everyone, impressions like that, but most people ignore them. If you pay attention to them, you get more control—"

"She sent my brother out to get me. I know you heard them talking about what I was doing!"

"Yes! I was getting ready to go. He came out of his room and your mama said, 'Go out there and get her. It isn't natural for a girl to just sit in the grass for hours looking into space.' Those were her exact words. I have a very good memory. Your brother said to leave you alone, and your mother nagged him until he went out. But nobody said a word about cats or graves. I swear on the blood of Jesus."

Sarah didn't know what to think. "I could ask my mother," she said.

"Yes, I know you could. Why don't you?"

"I might." Sarah picked up a dish towel and dried the glass Cissy had just washed. "Because I really think this stuff is all smoke and mirrors."

"That's your privilege. I won't mention it again if you don't want me to."

"No, I don't want you to . . . well, why don't you tell me some more, and then I can evaluate what you're saying?"

"No pressure, huh?" Cissy grinned. "Okay. Like I said, I looked at you and I saw the black cat. I know . . . she was your cat for a long time, since you were a little girl. And she died recently and she feels . . . protective toward you . . . she wants to stick close to you un- til . . ." Cissy's eyes were changing, focusing inward.

Sarah leaned forward. "Until what?"

Cissy looked into the suds. Her fingers tightened on the edge of the sink. "I think maybe there's some kind of trouble . . . danger . . . something that's been coming for a long time. For years. And it's building up now, it's going to happen soon . . . bad, lots of . . . I don't know . . . blood? I can feel your cat . . . she wants to stay here and help until it's over. Did you make a deal with her or something? She feels bound to help you." She looked up, blinking. "That's something I never did before."

"What?"

"Get into the feelings of an animal."

"You heard my cat say those things?"

"No . . . not in words. She's here . . . somewhere. . . . I can see her feelings. It's hard to explain. I've done it with people on the other side, but never an animal. I didn't know until this minute that they . . . go on after death. You know?"

Sarah didn't know. She wanted to believe this more than anything. She looked away but was confronted by thousands of mirror images of Cissy's face reflected in the black tile backsplash. Was it a good face or an evil face?

"I'm really not telling you right," said Cissy. "Some of this stuff is hard to describe, and I see it quickly, sometimes, in flashes. What I really have been seeing is a black silhouette of a cat. Like a shadow."

Sarah felt cold. "What?"

"I'm seeing the shadow of a cat. But I still know it's a black cat anyway. I can't describe."

Sarah stared into Cissy's green eyes. They had a

depth you could get lost in if you weren't careful. A soap bubble drifted between them, then burst.

"My cat's *name* was Shadow," Sarah said.

"Oh," Cissy said softly. "I've seen things like that before. The way they communicate sometimes. Well, I've seen it with dead . . . people. They almost make a word-picture in my mind. It's spooky, though, to think an animal would do that. But then the whole thing is spooky. The whole world."

For the first time in her life, Sarah thought maybe that was true.

That night Sarah dreamed about Shadow. First it was a beautiful dream. They were sitting together in the sunshine. Shadow was in Sarah's lap, butting her head against Sarah's stomach. Sarah could feel the warmth and weight of her. She felt the heat of the sun in Shadow's fur. The cat looked up, and Sarah gazed into her intelligent jade eyes, knowing for just a minute that they were communicating without thoughts. They were together.

The sky was crayon-blue with soft little puffs of cloud, but then something went wrong. A fissure appeared in the blueness, then widened. A piece of the sky broke loose and fell, crashing near Sarah's leg, shattering like glass.

Shadow's body tensed: Sarah could feel the cat's leg muscles bracing, preparing to leap away. She held Shadow tighter, more protectively. "It's okay," Sarah said. But Shadow was gazing up at the sky, looking terrified.

There was a jagged black hole where the piece had fallen out. New fissures and cracks were spreading over the whole surface.

Suddenly chunks of glass were raining down, all around them, smashing, tinkling. The air grew dark as the blue sky was replaced by a black one. Shadow panicked, twisting in Sarah's arms, struggling to get away. Sarah tried to clamp down on her, leaning over to shield the cat's body with her own. A huge piece of glass struck Sarah, breaking over her back.

Shadow growled. Her claws slashed out, raking Sarah's arm. Sarah let go, and Shadow bounded away, sprinting off through the rain of broken glass.

It was very dark. Most of the sky was gone. Shadow had disappeared into the gloom. Sarah sat paralyzed and sad, staring at her arm where the thin lines of blood trickled like streams of red wine.

Four

Things happened to Sarah in the dark. Even in semidarkness, such as a movie theater, she would begin to have feelings and strange thoughts. It never bothered her, but she knew it was the kind of thing a smart person would keep to herself. For instance, sitting next to Julian in the movies now, she felt the essence of him sitting there. It was something strong, massive, rocklike, violet in color. Julian had a soul that was steady, didn't jump around, stayed where it belonged.

Unlike the girl in front of them, who had fanned her streaked-blond hair over the seat back. Her essence was tipping and tilting dangerously, although she sat motionless. In her Sarah saw something like a spinning coin when it begins to lose its rhythm and wobbles erratically. The girl had a color too. Orange, or no, gold, brassy gold, the color of corn oil. Somewhere in the theater Sarah felt someone who was jingly, like sleigh bells, and somewhere else she got the strong impression of hard, brittle transparent red, like candy. None of it made any sense to her, and she didn't really think about it much. It was in the part of her mind she paid little attention to, the rambling part, the part you had to abandon yourself to when you wanted to fall asleep or write a poem, but that most of the time you dismissed as crazy. Maybe this was what Cissy was talking about, those feelings you could cultivate and develop.

Now she was listening attentively, because something heavy and serious was coming through. Something incongruous with the pretty, watercolor London on the screen, full of bouncy puppies and handsome men with pipes and sweater vests.

Sarah had picked up something spooky in the theater.

No, *spooky* didn't cover it. It was something awesome, huge and powerful, like a storm. It had a grandeur that lured her mind away from the puppies on screen and the warm comfort of Julian's presence.

It was cold. It was like an attic or a cave that drew you, even though you were afraid of what might be inside. Just like that. Sarah closed her eyes, but that made the feeling recede, so she opened them again. The shadows in the theater contributed to it. And the sound of the projector under the soundtrack, the whir that everyone could hear but that most of the audience was screening out. Sarah tipped her head back and looked up at the beam of light from the projectionist's booth.

There was a bump inside the whir, if you listened. It was *whir-bump, whir-bump.* A universe of dust and particles swirled in the platinum light beam. Sarah felt suddenly huge and powerful, the way she sometimes felt when cloud watching. She felt that with very little effort she could ascend and swirl in that chaotic white wind and join it and lose Sarah altogether and just be part of the whirling whiteness, join it, and . . .

Just beyond the beam of light there it was, projected on the ceiling of the theater. The shadow of a beautiful, sinuous cat, stretching the whole length of the theater ceiling. Pointed ears, whiskers, delicately tapered throat.

Sarah was mesmerized, afraid to look away. *Something that happens to be shaped like a cat*, she told herself. *An illusion from the light beam. It's the edge of a seat or a box of popcorn magnified ten million times. It's not my cat. I'm not the only one who can see this.*

Then the shadow moved, tilted its head just a fraction. An unmistakable animal movement. It appeared to have cocked its head to look directly at Sarah.

Scared now, Sarah jabbed Julian's arm.

"What?" he said in a voice a million miles away. Was he looking up? Did he see her, staring at the ceiling? Would he know enough to look up and see what she was seeing?

"What?" he repeated, and she knew he was still looking at the movie, only giving her half his attention.

The shadow on the ceiling compressed, then expanded suddenly. A cat leaping . . . somewhere. The shadow was gone. Sarah stared crazily at the white whirl of light from the projection booth, feeling her muscles relax and let go. Her neck was stiff and sore.

Whir-bump, whir-bump, whir-bump.

On the screen the Dalmatians were struggling through the snow, carrying puppies in their mouths. Julian had leaned forward in his seat, mentally helping the puppies make it to safety. Sarah took his hand, for once not worried about looking too obvious. His hand was strong and warm, like a chunk of granite heated in the sun.

"Do you believe in ghosts?" Sarah asked as she further stomped down her fears by stuffing hot fudge and whipped cream in her mouth.

"That's not a good question." Julian stirred his sundae with a precise rhythm as he sought to reduce all the elements in it to a pale chocolate soup. "I believe in the various phenomena that are attributed to ghosts, but I think there are different explanations for each of those."

Sometimes Sarah got a little sick of him. "Do you think the dead come back and haunt us?"

He looked up at her angry tone. "Probably not."

She took another big mouthful. She was almost at the bottom of her parfait glass and they'd just started eating five minutes ago. "Okay. So all these people who say they've seen ghosts, what are they seeing?"

"This is an interesting subject," Julian said. He looked down for a minute to correct his stirring. "I mean, I don't think people are lying when they say these things happen. They believe what they're experiencing is real."

"But . . ." Sarah prompted.

"But . . . I think people don't realize how powerful the mind is. I think, I mean, we know it can create whole hallucinations just because some little wire gets crossed or some chemical runs low. People think just because they perceive something, that it's real. But not necessarily."

Sarah considered this for a minute. "But you can't be sure of that. Maybe some people really see more than others. You know?"

He licked off his spoon and stirred some more. "Well, what I'd say is, does this person who sees something have a psychological reason for *wanting* to see it? I'll give you an example. One time my parents sent me off for a summer to be with my aunt in Los Angeles. Okay? I was really sad and homesick. You know what I kept seeing? My family. I'd see my dad in a crowd buying a newspaper. I'd see my mom getting on a bus. I'd see a car just like ours out in traffic. 'Cause that's what I was looking for in my mind. Get it?"

Sarah sighed. "So if someone dies and somebody sees a ghost, you think it's just because they miss the dead person?"

"Bingo." Julian had now effectively sludged his sundae and looked up again. "Why are you asking this stuff?"

Sarah felt like a deer caught in headlights. "I don't know."

He frowned. When he was serious, his dark eyes were especially beautiful. "Sarah, tell me."

"You'll think I'm crazy."

"I already do," he said with a straight face.

Sarah giggled. Then she sobered up for the confession. "I think I'm seeing images of Shadow all around."

There was a long pause. His eyes didn't even react. When he finally spoke, his voice was low. "You took it so hard. . . ."

"So you think I'm just manufacturing this stuff to keep her alive, right? Everything is always in my head. It couldn't possibly be real."

"I don't know, Sarah. I'm not God or anything. I don't know everything. But you went through a bad thing and now it's back. The first place I would look would be inside your own head. Don't you think so too?"

"Yeah, but I don't want to think I'm going crazy."

"That wouldn't be crazy. That would be normal. Lots of people see things and hear things. My family is Catholic. They believe in everything. When somebody dies, you can bet one of my aunts or somebody will see them in a dream or get a message. It just makes everyone feel better. It's not crazy. It's just how your mind helps you cope with bad stuff. But you shouldn't believe in it, that's how you get crazy. See?"

Sarah had finished her ice cream and was looking hungrily at Julian's untouched slop. "What if your aunts are all psychic? What if they can see things you can't see? Maybe because your mind is closed, you're missing something."

"My mind isn't closed. I'm a scientist. My mind is wide open. Nobody knows anything for sure. I'm just telling you what makes the most sense to me. I think you see what you want to see."

"Our housekeeper is psychic. She told me Shadow was still around, waiting to help me with something."

"Maybe your housekeeper is just perceptive enough to see what's on your mind and exploit it, Sarah."

"Why do I want to disagree with you?" Sarah cried. He looked down as if she'd reproached him. "Because you're scared of death, like all the rest of the world. So you make up stories to protect yourself. If Shadow didn't die, then you don't have to die either."

"Don't you think our spirit goes somewhere when we die?" Sarah begged.

"I think the energy from our bodies disseminates peacefully into the universe," he said happily.

Sarah pushed her ice cream away. She felt sick.

To My First Child Upon Her Death

Lost, I'm lost
My hands reach out
For fur, for fire-green eyes
My lap has lost the weight and warmth
The needles in my thighs
Walk, I walk
but now the path
is lonely, cold and dead
My joy, my friend, my childhood's end
A shadow in my head

Sarah hadn't looked at the poem since the funeral. Patrick had told her it was a requiescat and they laughed over the pun. She even thought of changing the title to "Requies-Cat," but she thought that cheapened it. It was an interesting poem when you looked at it now. Was Shadow haunting her head? Should she tell her parents and get counseling, as she was sure Dear Abby would urge her to do? Maybe that was the wise thing.

She tried to look back through the dense silver-black fog that seemed to surround the events of last summer.

The little problems with Shadow, the trips to the vet.

Vomiting. All the theories. She got a bad lizard. She drank from a puddle. She swallowed some yarn. Sarah's father's voice like a clock striking: "We'd better let the vet run those tests."

Cancer of the stomach. Now it had a name. A very, very bad name.

Different medicines. Antiemetics, appetite enhancers. Shadow hated them all. Sarah felt cruel forcing liquids into the struggling cat's mouth. No way to explain these were acts of love.

Weight checks. Eight pounds. Seven pounds. Six pounds. Dr. Metzger's voice. "I'm not sure there's much more we can do."

Diets. Baby food. Lamb and rice. Spoon-feeding. Dropper-feeding. Incontinence. Messes and smells. Passing blood. Listlessness.

Sarah had never dealt with helplessness before. She was a goal setter. Everything she'd ever done in life had been a matter of applying energy and seeing progress. That was how she thought life worked. She hadn't realized there was another side, where the bad thing pushes you down relentlessly, no matter how you struggle.

Clinging to hope. Sarah's voice. "She ate a little more today. I think." People looking away, not answering. Desperation. Prayers. Promises to God, the Catholic church, Saint Francis. Superstition. *When I wear blue, she tends to eat more. If it rains this morning, she'll start to get better.*

Shadow looking into Sarah's eyes, asking for something. Was it *Save me*? Or *Help me die*? It was Sarah's decision alone. She remembered the moment she made the decision, after that last conference with the vet. As soon as she made it, she felt the weight come down on her chest like an avalanche of stones.

It was getting warm in the room. She opened the windows and let the spring breeze dry the sweat on her face. The yard smelled faintly of jasmine. The sun was going down. Sarah had skipped dinner, stayed in her room, claiming the ice cream had spoiled her appetite. Her brothers were in the hall now arguing. "You suck!" "*You* suck!" A door slammed. So much for talking this over with Patrick. Sarah rolled over and held the blank book above her head, seeing how the poem read from this new perspective. She didn't want Julian to be right. She didn't want the shadows around her to be her imagination. But wanting that proved his point, didn't it?

"Let me in that room, you little shit!" Pounding and kicking.

"Fuck off."

"I mean it! When I get in there, I'm gonna kick your worthless little ass!"

"Go hang by your feet!"

"Mom!"

"What in the devil is going on here? Are both of you six years old?"

"He locked me out of our room!"

"It wasn't locked, he's too stupid to open it!"

"I don't want to hear any more of this! Your sister is sick. Don't you have any consideration?"

"Can't he sleep in the garage? I don't want him in here!"

"It was my room first, you little—"

"That's enough, and I mean it. Unless you want your father to get involved in this, and I don't think you do.

Patrick, you are not allowed to lock Brian out. If you do that again, we'll have to take the locks off the door. Okay?"

"Whatever."

Her footsteps receded down the hall.

A dull, heavy thud. "Ow! You piece of—"

"Don't you try anything like that again, faggot, or you'll wake up with a pillow over your face."

"At least I wouldn't have to look at you! Don't!"

Sarah sighed and went to the window. Twilight. The breeze lifted and teased the cypress fronds. The scent of jasmine was strong. Sarah was nocturnal. She always felt somehow relieved when the sun went down. She took several deep breaths of the night air and shut out the sounds of her brothers pummeling each other. She waited for the Quiet.

A few pinpoints of light appeared in the sky. Sarah gazed at them, listening to the wind rattling the palm tree in the side yard, a sound you couldn't even describe to a northerner. As the blue deepened across the yard, Sarah began to feel free again. Something inside her felt elated, like running and prancing in the grass. Julian was wrong. There was something else to this world, something wild and unpredictable, an element of magic.

"Shadow?" she whispered to the darkness. "If you are really here, come to me right now. Let me see you or hear you so I can know you're really here."

She waited, rigid and still for any sign, any shadows, any rustle of the grass. There was a dog barking somewhere. A car went down the street. The wind died down. Nothing. Sarah closed the window.

She decided to handle this the way she often handled

difficult questions. She would take a survey. She went back to the bed and opened her blank book to the next clean page and numbered it. Beside number 1 she wrote *Patrick* and then hesitated, trying to simplify what he'd said on the subject. *Death is an illusion like everything else. Number 2. Cissy—ghosts are real. Number 3. Julian—it's all in your head.* Okay, two to one, not that bad. She would ask her mother and father and . . . maybe Brian, although she didn't have much respect for his opinion.

Her door opened, and her mother came in with a dish of tapioca. "Feeling better?" she asked. She sat on the bed, tucking one leg under her. She handed the dish to Sarah, sweeping her hair back with her free hand. Sarah loved to watch her mother do things because she was graceful. Patrick was the only one who'd caught that gene.

"Yeah. Much better. Mom? I'm doing a paper on attitudes and beliefs in the nineties. Will you help me?"

"Sure."

"What are your beliefs about life after death?"

"Honestly?"

"Honestly."

Mrs. Shaheen took a little breath and then let it out in a half sigh, half laugh. "I think when you're dead, you're dead like a chicken." ·

Sarah stopped eating. "Okay, thanks."

"That's what I really think. You asked. Don't tell your father, though. He might want to discuss it with me."

"Thanks for the pudding, Mom."

"Is that all you're going to eat?"

"I think so."

"Maybe I should keep you home tomorrow."

"Yeah, maybe."

"Sleep tight, Pixie."

"Okay."

On her way down the hall Mrs. Shaheen rapped on the boys' door. "That's more like it," she called to them.

"Good night, Mom!" They chorused sweetly.

"I hate you!" Brian added when she was out of earshot.

"I hate you more!" Patrick insisted.

Sarah sighed and picked up her book. She wrote, *4. Mom—chicken.*

Five

Sarah rolled onto her stomach, feeling the sun burn into her back. Summer was her favorite season, when everything in nature was alive and close. Through the green-and-white webbing of her deck chair she could gaze down into a jungle; spears of grass bending under the march of a palmetto bug, tiny chartreuse moths hovering over heather blossoms, ancient lizards motionless, except for their slow, scarlet throat display. She breathed in the rich mixture of scents, trying to isolate each element. Freshly cut grass. Hot soil. Jasmine. Cypress. Coconut oil (that was Patrick, sleeping in the other chair, working on his tan). Spandex (that was Sarah, wearing a brand-new two-piece, pink with orange daisies). Something else, something tantalizing, like meat. Someone must be cooking out.

She realized this was her first relaxed moment in a whole week. In the seven days since Brian had come home the tension in the house had been rising steadily.

Brian was wounded on all fronts, trying to call an angry Karen, who kept hanging up on him, dodging his father's attempts to get him a summer job in the hospital where Dr. Shaheen practiced, trying to live down the shame of his grades while Patrick spent the week acing all his final exams. When Brian was suffering, he made sure everyone around suffered with him. "He's like a bear with a sore foot," Mrs. Shaheen was fond of saying. Patrick seemed all wound up, too, pacing, fidgeting, trying not to notice that the Shaheens were downplaying his academic performance so that Brian wouldn't feel bad. Cissy was a mysterious wild card in this, adding a weird, disturbing element. She hung up bunches of herbs all over the kitchen and sometimes burned incense. She made cryptic remarks, as if she knew a lot more about everything than she was telling. Sarah found her alluring and frightening at the same time. On top of all this Sarah was troubled about the shadow she'd seen at the movies. She wanted a definite explanation, but she didn't like any of the explanations she could think of. It came down to the fact that she was either cracking up and seeing things or she was really being haunted by a dead cat. Who wanted a choice like that?

Patrick was sitting up now, reading something called *The Drunken Boat*. He was always reading books Sarah had never heard of but he insisted were classics.

"Trick?" Sarah said. Her voice sounded nervous and childish even to herself.

He pushed his sunglasses up through his fine hair so that they could make eye contact. "Uh-huh?"

"How would a person know if they were crazy?"

He laughed. "Do you think you are?"

"I'm asking you a serious question."

"All thirteen-year-olds think they're crazy. Come to think of it, most of them are. But it's temporary."

"I'm really trying to talk here."

"I'm sorry, sweetie, but I'm not worried. You're a level headed little child. You're the last person I would suspect of insanity. Now, my other sibling . . . I could easily see him wielding a chain saw, but not you. You're saner than me, and of course"—he dropped his voice into the Boris Karloff range—"I'm perfectly normal." He laughed maniacally.

"Okay. Don't talk to me."

"I'm sorry. Go ahead."

She lifted her chin, almost determined to prove there was something wrong now. "I'm having hallucinations."

Something in his eyes changed. "Of what?"

"I thought I saw a shadow of a cat in the movies last week."

"Like a shadow of Shadow?"

"Yes."

"Well . . . I'm not sure that's an hallucination. If Shadow came over and had a conversation with you wearing a top hat and tails, then I'd call a doctor. But how do we know? I mean, how do we know what's really out there?" He gestured toward the sky. "Maybe we can see back in time or forward in time. I don't understand physics, but I read in some book that time isn't really like a flowing river, it's like a dimension that's sort of curving and spiraling around us. You hear about people who go to a Civil War battlefield and see the battle happening. Maybe they're just seeing the ghost of the past. Maybe people who see UFOs are seeing the future.

Who knows? I think sometimes we dismiss these things too quickly."

Sarah liked the time concept. But she couldn't see how it applied to her experience. Shadow had never hung out in movie theaters. "The way it seems to me," she said, choosing her words carefully, "is that Shadow is here, right here, only in some kind of different form or dimension, and she wants me to see her." Sarah almost held her breath, waiting to see how he'd react to that.

His eyes searched hers. Then he looked at the middle distance for a second. He was giving it thought. He didn't dismiss it out of hand. "I've always thought you might be especially sensitive to things like this," he began.

Suddenly Brian seemed to come out of nowhere. Sarah should have seen him coming, but her eyes had been focused on Patrick, screening out everything else.

Brian swooped up behind Patrick and smacked the back of his head. "Hi, Patsy! Is this just a girls' party, or can anybody join in?"

Sarah was furious with him. She might never get Patrick in the proper mood to discuss this subject again. "You can only sit here if you're nice and polite and don't insult people!" she challenged.

"Yes, ma'am. I'm sorry." He gave her a little salute. Brian behaved for Sarah. It was a mystery to her, but it was true. He settled himself in the third deck chair. "What's the topic of discussion?"

"Whether Mom should have had an abortion nineteen years ago," Patrick said, exploring the back of his head with his fingers.

Sarah turned to him. "You have to be nice too. Can't

the two of you ever think of anything to do but compete? It's boring!"

"What fag book is that?" Brian inquired of Patrick. "Something about sailors on leave?"

"I'm going in the house," Patrick threatened, although he didn't move.

"Settle down, I'm just playing. Give me the suntan stuff, would you?"

Patrick threw it at Brian's face, but Brian raised his hand and caught it neatly. "Listen," he said. "I agree with Sarah. This stuff is getting boring. Let's call a truce for the afternoon. I can't get my stupid girlfriend to talk to me on the phone, so I haven't got anything to do tonight. You want to go to the drive-in tonight? Like old times?"

"Oh, yes!" Sarah cried. She could remember vividly, when Brian first got his driver's license, how he would take the three of them out to the TwinStar on State Road 7. They would find the goriest horror pictures and eat as much junk as they could hold. During these times the three of them were united, mocking and making fun of every aspect of the B-movies, exchanging cruel comments about the people around them, acting as little like intelligent, well-brought-up kids as they could. It was a vacation from their true identities. "You know what we could see? *The Hand That Rocks the Cradle.* That's the one where the evil baby-sitter—"

"Rebecca De Mornay!" Brian interjected.

"She takes over the house, and everyone trusts her, and then—"

"Don't tell it if we're going to go!" Patrick said.

"I'll tell you, if I had Rebecca De Mornay for a baby-sitter, she could do any unspeakable thing to me she wanted," Brian said.

"Okay, don't drool," Sarah said. She turned to Patrick. "Would you go?"

He looked grudgingly at Brian. Then he half smiled. "Are you going to buy us corn dogs?" he asked.

Brian smiled back genuinely. "Sure."

"Okay, I'm not doing anything anyway." Patrick dropped his sunglasses down and stretched out, as if exhausted from being civil to Brian.

Sarah gave Brian a smile of approval.

"Right around back here." Cissy's voice rang out. "All three of them."

"Thanks!" It was Karen's voice. She appeared around the side of the house wearing a pink-checked shorts set trimmed in white eyelet. A little too babyish for Sarah's taste. She wore cat's-eye sunglasses and had enhanced her mouth with a slash of coral. Brian's first impulse was to sit up, then he seemed to realize that was wrong and slumped down. Patrick covered his lap with his open book. Sarah noted all this with amusement. The effect women had on men never failed to amaze her.

"Hi, kids!" Karen said, like the star of a beach-party movie walking into her first scene.

Brian was now affecting so much cool, he looked slightly ill. "How's it going?" he mumbled.

"Hi," said Patrick, looking off into the trees.

Sarah didn't bother with a greeting.

"This is my kind of weather!" Karen said, still sounding like an actress on stage. She took a big, lazy arm stretch, which captured the attention of both boys. Then she did a remarkable thing. She sat down on the end of *Patrick's* deck chair. He jerked his legs to the right to avoid making contact. A faint blush seeped across his face.

Brian didn't react visibly, but his voice became wary. "I was about to call you," he said.

"Were you?" Karen turned to Sarah. "How are you doing? Is your school out now?"

Sarah didn't like being used as a prop in this play. "One more week."

"Write any poems lately?"

Sarah sniffed. "I write poems all the *time*."

Patrick was now in the process of trying surreptitiously to pull his knees up, apparently to avoid any accidental contact with Karen's body. Sarah had never seen him look so uncomfortable. He was now using his book as a chest guard.

"I'm sorry about last Saturday," Brian said gruffly. "You know me and my mouth."

"I sure do," Karen said. She turned around to look at Patrick. "You're looking good," she said. "You've been getting a lot of sun."

"I try," he said softly.

Sarah was beginning to see where this was going. She sat up.

"How'd you do on your finals?"

"Oh, you know. Aced them. I'm a pretty boring guy." Patrick was beginning to look less shy.

"You got straight A's?" Her coral-painted hand touched his knee. "You're kidding."

"He cheats," Brian said. The tone of his voice was about the same as that of a police officer saying, "Drop that gun."

"I had easy courses this semester," Patrick went on as if his brother hadn't spoken. "Theater and—"

"You were great in *The Bad Seed*. I never got around to telling you."

"Typecasting," Brian muttered.

Patrick ignored him. "Thanks. It's not my favorite play, but you don't always get to pick them. At least I got a good part."

"Well, of course you did," she smiled, her hand now swiveling on his knee. "Everybody knows you're the best actor in the school."

"Do you want a Coke or a beer or anything?" Brian asked loudly.

"No, thanks." She didn't look around. "Are you going to try to be a professional actor?"

"Oh, I don't know. That's kind of a crazy, hopeless thing to want, isn't it? I guess I'll give it a shot, but I know I have to have something real planned to back it up."

Now her fingers squeezed; a knee hug. "Well, with your grades you could obviously do anything."

Brian was beginning to breathe harder, the way children do when they're working themselves up to a tantrum or a crying jag.

"Is your family going on a vacation this year?" Sarah asked Karen, trying to get the conversation back to the four of them, instead of this one-on-one.

Karen finally let go of Patrick's knee. "Yeah, I guess we have to go camping. Everybody likes it but me. Ugh.

Going to the bathroom outdoors, walking through spiderwebs. It's like a horror movie."

"I wish we'd go camping sometime," Sarah said.

Patrick laughed. "Fat chance. Can you see Mom in the wilderness? Trying to plug in her blow dryer?"

"I don't exactly picture *you* as Davy Crockett either," Brian said.

Patrick laughed. "That's true," he said happily. "I'm a sissy. My idea of roughing it is a hotel with no room service." He and Karen laughed together.

Sarah was amazed. Never in her life had she seen Patrick be mature about Brian's teasing. Something astonishing had happened here, some major shift. And all because a girl had put her hand on his knee.

"I was wondering, Patrick," said Karen. "Since Brian doesn't like picnics all that much and I really do . . . and since your mother thinks you ought to socialize more"—she paused and smiled while he laughed—"I was just wondering if you'd like to go on a little picnic with me next week. I love to cook and I'd make us some fantastic food. Want to?"

Sarah looked at Brian. He wasn't moving at all. He sat as still as if a gun were trained on him.

Patrick cleared his throat. "Sure. That'd be great."

Karen turned to Brian. "Well, we solved that problem," she told him. "Now you're really off the hook."

Brian got up without a word and went into the house.

Everyone observed a moment of silence.

"Well . . ." Karen said. "I don't see why he thinks he has the right to be angry when he didn't want to go with me."

"I don't either," Patrick said. He turned to Sarah. "Right?"

"I guess so," Sarah said.

"What's a good day for you?" Karen asked Patrick. "Tuesday?"

"I don't know. I'm going out Monday to look for a job and I don't know what my schedule will be. I'll call you."

"Okay. You have my number?"

He smiled. "I'm sure it's around the house somewhere."

"I'll drive. Anything special you'd like me to wear?"

He blushed again. "I don't care. You look nice in that color you've got on."

She smiled slowly. "Do I?"

Sarah wished she weren't there.

"You look fantastic in that color," Patrick said quietly.

"You're sweet," she said. She took his chin in her hand and leaned forward, kissing his mouth gently. Her breasts grazed his knuckles, which were still clinging to the poetry book. "Gotta go!" she said, jumping up. " 'Bye, Sarah!"

" 'Bye," Sarah said.

Karen trotted off, the seat of her shorts bouncing rhythmically. Patrick stared until she disappeared around the side of the house. Then he turned to Sarah.

"What do you think?" he asked breathlessly. "Parallel universe?"

"Gotta be," she said.

"Well, whatever." He smiled crookedly. "Anyway, there's finally some justice in the world."

"Well, maybe."

"What do you mean?"

"Well . . . you know. I mean, she might be doing this for Brian's benefit."

"Oh, thanks! Like nobody would ever want to go out with me just because I'm a wonderful, charming guy!"

"Well, sure they would. But, you know, you're a year younger than her. . . ."

"So?"

"I don't know. You know how crazy she's always been about Brian. Then they have a fight and . . . obviously, this is a great way to get back at him. I mean, he's probably in your room right now stabbing your bed with the letter opener."

"Yeah!" Patrick said with satisfaction. "Okay, maybe she's doing that, but maybe not. I mean, isn't it just possible that from hanging around here she finally noticed I'm a nice human being and he's a total son of a bitch?"

"Maybe. Hey! *You* aren't just doing this to get Brian, are you?"

He sat up straighter. "What are you talking about? Have you looked at that girl? Or do you have your doubts about me like everybody else in the family?"

"No! Of course not. But . . ."

He gestured with his book, waving it. "Does everything that happens in this world have to be about Brian?"

"No, no."

"Well, it seems like it is. Haven't you ever noticed I'm much better-looking than him?"

"Sure you are, but—"

"So there you go. Look, this had to happen. First I went past him academically. Now I'm branching out into other arenas. Sooner or later he's just going to have to concede that I'm a superior person in every way. And then he'll simply have to get off the earth."

Sarah sighed. "As long as you're being realistic about it."

The bedroom window opened with a crash. "And don't think I'm taking either one of you little shits to the movies either!" Brian shrieked. The window slammed shut.

Patrick chuckled to himself.

Six

Sarah waited for Julian to catch up. He had his freezer bags out again and was wielding his pocket knife in the saw grass, taking a sample for the vast laboratory that was his bedroom.

"One of these days a 'gator's gonna get you while you're futzing around like that!" Sarah called.

"They're attracted to noises and sudden movements," he replied without looking up. "So I figure you're drawing all of them away from me."

"Ha-ha-ha." While she waited, Sarah sat down in the grass, imagining with delight her mother's shriek of horror. Mrs. Shaheen thought you could get chigger bites from sitting in the grass and hemorrhoids from sitting on sidewalks. And splinters from wooden benches. She was loads of fun at family picnics.

Sarah looked at the sky. The clouds gave mixed messages; white and black stirred together, edged in bright gold. The wind gathered them slowly into tall towers.

Sarah lifted her legs and did a shoulder stand, admiring her fuchsia and silver shoelaces.

"Okay, quit horsing around. I'm here," Julian said. "Jeez, do you have to put on a display like that?"

Sarah noted that he was straining to get a glimpse of the display despite his protests. She wondered if the leg of her shorts was wide enough that he could see her underwear. It was pink, to match her earrings and her shoelaces. Sarah loved having everything match. She let her legs fall, then stood, picking loose grass from her hair. Julian was looking away, eyes lowered. Interesting, interesting. "What did you find?" she asked.

"Huh?"

"Your sample, Stupid. What did you get?" She nudged his Ziploc bag.

"Oh! *Verbena tamensis.* The vervain. Here, smell." He broke the seal and held the open bag under her nose. A sweet, grandmotherly scent rose from the little mauve clusters.

"It's so pretty." Sarah cupped her hand under the bag.

"It's a natural emetic."

"Huh?"

"Makes you vomit."

"How special!" She drew back.

Julian looked up at the sky. "Is it going to rain?"

"It can't!" Sarah said. "We just got here. We have millions of things to do." Loxahatchee Wildlife Park was her favorite place on earth, a passion Julian shared. It was an immense playground for nature lovers; marsh trails like the one they were on, woodland walks, dioramas, ponds, and bridges. "Let's go to the observation tower!" Sarah said, tugging at Julian's hand.

"That's a good place to go when it looks like there might be lightning," he said, but he followed her. Sarah secretly thought he was excited by the fact that she talked him into doing reckless things.

They climbed the steep wooden stairs and gazed out over the acres of marsh. The first thing to do was always to look in the habitat pond for alligators. "There's a big guy right there," Julian said, pointing.

Sarah scanned the reeds and finally made out a series of bumps in the water. "What a hog!" she agreed.

"Purple gallinules," he said, his finger swinging to other quadrants. "Cormorants. Cattle egret. Wish we could spot a heron."

"Mmm-hmm." Sarah took note of the birds, but her attention was focused on the sky, where the cloud directly over the sun had developed a wicked black center. The wind was running in delicious streams over her face and through her hair. She picked up the leaden scent of ozone.

Julian was lost in cataloguing. "Teal ducks. See that? What are they doing around here? Must be passing through. There's a smaller 'gator off to the left. . . ."

People were beginning to vacate the trails now, looking up at the clouds. Cypress fronds fluttered and danced. The air grew dark and greenish. Distant sounds amplified; 'gators honking, birds trilling and tooting, cars in the parking lot revving up to go home. Then a rolling bass rumble that ended in a fierce crackle.

"Yikes!" Julian said, regaining his wits. He scanned

the sky like a surgeon reading an X ray. "I told you! Let's get the heck out of here."

"No!" Sarah cried. "Let's stay here. This is cool."

He furrowed his brow. "This is not cool. This is the highest point in the marsh. This is a wood tower. It could catch fire."

"That won't happen! What are the odds of that happening? There are tall trees over there!"

"That's a mile away from here! Come on, Sarah. I bet in a minute some ranger's going to shoo us out anyway. This is real bad."

Chartreuse flashed in the black clouds, followed by a loud boom. The wind began to whine. "Oh, please!" Sarah moaned, holding the wood railing and leaning out into the wind. "This is so cool!"

"You lunatic!" Julian wailed. "The storm is right over us. Come on!"

"No. You go. I want to feel the whole storm from up here."

"I can't leave you here, and you know it. You . . ." He apparently couldn't say the word he had in mind. "I figured you'd kill me someday!" he complained as he joined her at the rail.

"You'll love this!" Sarah assured him. She closed her eyes to feel the wet, green-smelling wind better. Little pockets of chill edged the warm rush of it. The darkness behind her eyelids flashed red, followed by a crash that surged adrenaline into her blood.

"Ai-yi-yi," Julian muttered.

Sarah opened her eyes. Forks of lightning tore into the dark clouds around them. The air boomed as if rockets and bombs were exploding. She could feel the sizzle and zap of energy spurting on the wind. It made her feel as if she could let go of the splintery wood railing and fly, go up herself like a glittery pink Roman candle and shoot sparks over the whole world.

Julian pointed to the west. "Look at that," he said.

The sky in that direction was a luscious violet. Against that rich backdrop, a wall of rain was driving toward them. Sarah had never seen rain move horizontally through space like this, but that was just what it was doing. A curtain of silver spangles rolling along, closer and closer, and then it was drumming on the wood roof of their shelter.

Julian let out a long breath. "Show's over," he said. He was right. The storm was moving away, rumbling like distant guns. Now they were left under a green-purple sky and a torrent of rain. The air was still and very cool.

"See?" Sarah said. "We didn't die."

He sat down on the wood planking, looking drained. "No, you crazy lunatic. We didn't die. I'm fourteen years old and I've got gray hair now, but we didn't die."

Sarah laughed at him and slid down in a sitting position next to him, wedged against him in fact. "You enjoyed it. I saw your face."

"Maybe. But no more adventures for today, okay?"

"Okay. How long are we stuck here for?"

"Oh, probably an hour or so." He was already setting up camp, taking his collection of Ziplocs out of his backpack and spreading them in a neat semicircle. Next he took out a sheet of gummed labels and a black felt-tip pen and began labeling his cuttings with his round, precise script.

"Wish we had food." Sarah sighed. Food was forbidden in the park because it could encourage 'gator attacks or create ecological imbalance. "We should have had something before we came here."

"Yeah," he said, but he wasn't listening. He was squinting at his *Physalis longifolia*.

Sarah felt pleasantly drained after the excitement of the storm. She had an urge to put her head on Julian's shoulder, but that would probably be a mistake. "You know, if you were a romantic kind of a guy, you'd pick wildflowers to give to beautiful women like me instead of labeling them like specimens."

He looked up. "You want this?" he asked, holding up the bag. "It's highly toxic."

"Oh, shut up." She sighed. She reached into her own pack and took out a tiny blank book with a geode on the cover and jotted some impressions of the storm. *Funeral in the sky*, she wrote. *Thunder like the wheels of a hearse.* That was good, she decided. Later she'd work it into a poem. *Green, purple, rain like silver needles. Something about the wind. Screaming? Grieving? Wailing?* Soon she was so absorbed, she didn't even hear the drumming of the rain.

Later the sun came out again and glittered on the wet saw grass. Julian and Sarah put away their quiet pursuits and came down from the tower. "Where to now?" Julian asked, stretching.

Sarah considered. The air was already heating up. It was going to be another blazing afternoon. "The woods," she said.

"Do you want to leave and go get something to eat and come back?" he asked. "I know you were hungry before."

"No," Sarah said. "Let's do the woods for an hour or so and then we can go to Pizza Hut or someplace and pig out."

"Deal."

The woodland trails were as fascinating as the marsh trails, a series of elevated wooden bridges forming a complex maze through the dense hammocks. Every few yards information was posted on the flora and fauna, which Julian read slowly and thoughtfully. Sarah was bored with that and tended to run ahead, stopping now and then to let him catch up.

The Florida woods were dense and spongy, oozing with movement and color. Life was everywhere; Spanish moss swinging from the branches of trees, lichens filling every rotted crevice, insects swarming. The trails had a lot of blind curves, so there was always a surprise ahead. So far Sarah had discovered a huge pileated woodpecker, an exotic-looking lizard with scales like glass beads, and a swarm of electric-blue dragonflies hovering over a pool of swamp water. It was a perfect day for exploration. The rain had scared away most of the other humans, and the creatures of the hammock were especially active and bold. Sarah tiptoed along in the cool shadows, recording every impression for future poetry.

Suddenly she turned a corner, and her whole body tightened with fear. Right in front of her, almost hidden in shadows, peering over the top of the plank walkway, was a horrible troll! His grayish fingers were long and knobby, clinging to the boards. His eyes were narrowed in a wicked hate stare directed at Sarah. His nose was so long, it seemed to be melting into the planking. Sarah's mind was screaming, *THIS CAN'T BE! THIS CAN'T BE!*

She tried to call for Julian, but only air came out of her throat. The troll held her with his piercing, ugly gaze. She felt if she moved even an inch, it would charge forward, and she would go insane from fear.

A pair of hands gripped her suddenly from behind. The scream was freed from her throat, a hot, piercing yowl of terror, echoed by another scream from the person who had grabbed her. It was Julian. *Oh, Julian!* She clamped down on his arm and pointed to the dusky shadows where the little creature was still crouching, not moving or making a sound. "Look!" she wailed shrilly.

He shook her off angrily. "Cut it out. That's not funny. What are you trying to do, scare me to death? I can see what that is."

As soon as he said it, Sarah could see what it was too: a misshapen cypress knee. The lights and shadows fell just right on its knobs and twists to make a hideous little human face. "Oh, shit!" said Sarah. "I thought it was real."

Julian laughed. "They're gonna lock you up someday," he said, shaking his head.

Sarah walked slowly beside him until her heart was beating normally again.

The sights and sounds of the woods were too interesting for just an hour's exploration. Julian began to add to his collection again, and Sarah drifted ahead again, now fully recovered from the troll episode. They had taken a different turn from their usual one, and Sarah felt they were in the deepest part of the woods now. Everything was silent and still. If she walked slowly and quietly, she could hear things scuttling in the brush or splashing in the swamp. The foliage was so dense here, almost no sunlight pierced through, just a little fawn spot on the planking now and then. All the tension from before melted in this dark, still place, and Sarah sat down on a bench and breathed deeply, waiting for Julian to catch up.

But he didn't come.

Determined this time to be a rational being, Sarah glanced at her watch and waited another five minutes. Nothing. Usually he was no more than a few yards behind her. Sarah got up and walked back the way she had come, only there was a fork, and she didn't know which way was right.

Against her will her heart began to set up a little drumming rhythm. Julian was the trailblazer, the one with the sense of direction. There were innumerable forks and side paths in this woods. Left on her own, it would take Sarah hours to find her way to one of the trail exits. None of the trails was marked with maps or directions. *Just stupid information on insect larvae and stuff!* Sarah thought angrily.

Stay calm, she told herself. *You've looked like enough of a fool for one day.* She wanted to backtrack more and try to find him, but she knew if she took the wrong fork, it would make it hard for him to find her. And in this case he was the smart one. It was embarrassing, but Sarah knew the best thing to do was to shout, give him a direction. Whatever the mix-up, he couldn't be too far away.

"Julian!" she called out. Her voice sounded odd among the natural sounds in the forest. Something in the hammock was startled and rustled violently.

She waited patiently, but there was no answer. Was he joking around? Or was she being too timid and not shouting loudly enough?

"JULIAN!" she shouted. "HEY! WHERE ARE YOU?"

Nothing. Just a loon in the distance.

Sarah's heart pounded. This was bad. This could go on for hours. She tried not to panic, but the panic was pretty determined. There was something really scary about this. Even though she tried to be rational, part of her mind was screaming that she had come into some part of the forest where no rangers could find her, where she would wander around forever and never see another human again.

"HELP!" she screamed. "SOMEBODY PLEASE! HELP ME! PLEEEEEEEEASE!"

If Julian was horsing around, that would have made him stop. He was a clown, but he wasn't cruel. But nobody heard her. Her screams echoed slightly, like mockery.

Hot tears bubbled up and spilled out, blinding her. This wasn't fair! She hadn't gone that far ahead. She didn't deserve this. Real fears started to worm their way in now. There were a few dangerous animals in the hammock: alligators and poisonous snakes, bobcats. The proud little posters all around were only too happy to point that out. Some insect bit her on the back of the neck. She felt like a little, lost child. "I'm hungry," she wailed out loud. "I'm hungry and I'm tired and I want to go home!" She sat down on the planking, oblivious to splinters or spiders, and fought a powerful urge to cry.

She thought she heard a sound. Sarah lifted her head, and through a mist of tears and eyelash rainbows she saw Shadow, about a hundred yards away, sitting and facing her. As soon as she saw the cat, it stood, turned, and walked around one of the blind corners in the trail.

"I'm cracking up," Sarah said. "It's really true. I'm gonna have to tell my parents and they'll put me in some Shady Glen or something until I'm better." She felt almost good now that everything was so bizarre. "Maybe I'm not even lost in the woods!" she continued as if she had an invisible audience. "I'm probably home watching TV!" In this spirit of absurdity she felt much better. She got up and walked in the direction she thought the cat had gone, and sure enough, when she rounded the corner, there was Shadow again, sitting and waiting. Sarah began to walk toward the cat slowly, hoping it would stay and let her catch up. It occurred to her that maybe she wasn't completely hallucinating. There could, after all, be a black cat in the woods. Not Shadow but some black cat looking for shrews and mice. At least following it gave her something constructive to do instead of crying her eyes out and picturing herself in an institution.

The cat looked into Sarah's eyes, then took off again, choosing a fork to its left. Whatever the thing was, its resemblance to Shadow was amazing. It was the same size and weight, had the same semifluffy fur texture, not a speck of white anywhere. It wasn't stopping and starting now, it was trotting along the paths at a brisk pace, forcing Sarah to hurry along after it. It kept forking to the left, always the left, as if making some kind of circle. The sun seemed to be at a very different angle now; the cat was leading her on unfamiliar paths, in an unfamiliar direction. "Let me catch up with you!" Sarah called breathlessly as she went from a trot to a jog.

The cat glanced around at her voice and broke into a sprint, charging across a little footbridge.

"No!" Sarah called. She had begun to believe that somehow the cat was her only hope, that it was leading her to safety. She broke into a run, her black-and-fuchsia tennis shoes pounding over the bridge. There was more light now, more sunshine. Sarah's hope surged. She ran full tilt behind the streaking black cat. Suddenly the trees thinned and the sunlight burst into her face and she was out of the woods, not ten feet from the Information Center.

There was no cat anywhere.

Instead there was Julian surrounded by park attendants, talking and gesturing hysterically, obviously about to organize a search party.

"Hey!" Sarah called, waving. "I'm okay!"

"That's her!" Julian shrieked, joy and relief breaking across his face. He ran to her and then stopped awkwardly, not knowing what to do.

The look on his face was enough for Sarah. "I'm fine!" she said breathlessly. "I don't know how I got so far away from you."

"I called you and called you!" he cried. "Why do you have to go off by yourself like that!"

The park employees were heading back toward the

Information Center now, laughing together, probably about silly kids and puppy love.

"I won't do it anymore," Sarah said. "I really learned my lesson. I was so scared. I was thinking I'd be stuck in there forever."

"You'd last about ten minutes in the wilderness too!" he continued.

"I know," she said humbly. There was something kind of exciting about the way he was scolding her. She enjoyed it. And she had a feeling he was enjoying it, too, since he seemed to be prolonging it.

"I don't know how I ever got mixed up with a crazy little thing like you!"

"Just lucky, I guess," she said, smiling crookedly.

He lowered his voice, even though they were all alone. "Don't scare me like that again, Sarah, okay?" A little flush spread across his cheeks.

She lowered her voice too. "Okay," she said.

"Okay!" He pivoted quickly and headed for the bike rack. "We should be going. I know you're starving by now."

"Yes." She began to follow him. She wanted to tell him about what had happened, about Shadow, or whatever it was that was leading her out of the woods. She knew it was crazy, but Julian was her best friend, and she'd always told him everything.

They came to the bike rack. "One more thing," Julian said, digging into his pack. He took out the freezer bag with the vervain in it, extracted the little blossom, and held it out to her. "Here."

Sarah took it, startled. "What for?"

He threw his leg over his bike. "Who knows what for? Maybe I'm a romantic guy after all!" And he pedaled away, trusting her to follow and keep up.

Sarah decided she didn't have to tell him about Shadow right away.

Seven

Sarah loved to watch her father. Tonight he was balancing the checkbook, his hand gliding down the columns, ticking off items with a neat little flourish. The dining room chandelier cast a circle of warm light around him. He was the only peaceful person in the family, Sarah realized, the only one who wasn't continually striving to be noticed. Maybe because he didn't need to be.

Tonight it was just Sarah and her father. Mrs. Shaheen was working late at the newspaper. She said she could only concentrate when all the editors were gone.

Patrick had found a summer job on his first try, at a bookstore in the mall. He'd called to say he was working that very night and then asked Brian to come to the phone and give him Karen's number so that he could set up the picnic for tomorrow. Right after that, Brian had gone out for a walk, which was now in its third hour. Cissy was just finishing up in the kitchen.

Dr. Shaheen loved quiet. He worked with no radio or TV to distract him. Because of that, little house sounds filled the void: the whisper of the central air, the clank of pots and pans, the grumble of the icemaker. Sarah joined her father at the dining room table, opened her blank book, and uncapped her pen.

Dr. Shaheen looked up distractedly and smiled.

The blank book opened to the page where Sarah had pressed Julian's vervain blossom. Isis' Tears—that's what Cissy called it when Sarah had showed it to her. She said the voodoo queens down in the French quarter used it to make medicines and potions. Sarah jotted a note to write a love story someday and call it "Isis' Tears." She turned several pages through looking for past material that might be interesting. She hesitated over a poem, making brief editorial changes and noting some weak words that needed replacements. Then she came upon the survey she'd started a week ago. The poll on people's attitudes about death.

She needed her father's opinion. Of all the people Sarah knew, her father struck her as the most intelligent and rational.

"Daddy?" she said impulsively.

He looked up again. His pale-gray eyes looked startled. When he concentrated on something, it was as if he'd fallen asleep.

"When you get finished, could we have a talk?"

He closed his checkbook immediately. He was a victim of sitcoms about caring fathers who talked things over with their kids. "Go ahead, Pixie."

"Well . . ." Sarah twined her arms like vines, a gesture left over from childhood. "This is serious. I want to talk about . . . death."

He nodded.

Sarah took a deep breath. "Do you believe in life after death?"

"Yes, I do. I . . . I know it isn't fashionable, especially for a so-called Man of Science, but I have faith in religion. I think we must. I think we must believe in something greater than ourselves, or else we feel . . . lost. Everything becomes meaningless." He held out his hand, palm up, as if offering something. "I mean, look at what I do. What's the point of helping people get well if it isn't *for* anything? If we all die and blink out like candles, why should I bother?"

"Uh-huh," Sarah was scribbling. She wrote, *Faith in religion. Must believe. Lost, meaningless, not blink out like candles*. "Do you believe in heaven and hell?"

He bit his lip. "I hope God is kind. I don't want to contradict the tenets of the Church, but I hope whatever system is in place is . . . kind."

Sarah looked at him for several seconds and wrote, *Kind system*. "Do you believe in ghosts?"

"Yes, I do," he said emphatically. "I've seen them."

Sarah forgot to write. "What?"

"I saw a ghost once." He lowered his voice. "This was when I was just a boy, when my grandfather, Wills, died. I really loved him. I wish you could have known him. He was a storyteller. You might get some of your talent from him. I used to go to his house when I was fed up with my own parents, and he'd tell me the family history, or describe Civil War battles, or he'd just make up stories on the spot about dragons and knights or whatever I wanted."

"Wow," Sarah said. "You used to do that for us when we were little."

He smiled. "I was stealing Grampa Wills's material. I learned it all from him."

"So what about the ghost part?"

"Well, when he died, I was devastated. I didn't want to go to the funeral home and view the body, but my mother made me. I mean, I must have been twelve, I was really old enough to face up to death, but I loved this man so much . . . you know?"

"Sure."

"So, when I got there, I just . . . freaked out. I really did. Like that time when you and I and Patrick got stuck in the elevator and we found out Patrick had claustrophobia?"

Sarah giggled at the memory. "You were screaming and everything?" she asked.

"Yeah. But my mother was one of these people like . . . you have to do the right thing even if it kills you. I'll tell you a secret, Sarah. That's why we live in Florida. I had to get away from that woman."

Sarah laughed out loud. She found Grandma Shaheen a little overbearing too. "Does Mom know this?"

He nodded. "Anyway it's beside the point. My mother dragged me up to that coffin, and I was just holding in my screams with all the energy I could muster, but it was too much. Have you ever seen a corpse, Sarah?"

She drew back a little. "Not a person."

"Well, your first one is hard. I mean, look at me now. In med school I used to cut up cadavers and then go out for pizza. But the first time you see an . . . empty body. . . . That's what it is. Empty. No more soul. That's another thing that makes me believe in the immortality of the soul: the difference between a living body and a dead one. You can sure see something has moved out. Anyway . . . I went nuts in that solemn place. My mom was fit to be tied. She dragged me off to a little side room . . . some kind of a coffee room or something, and she slapped my face and told me to quit embarrassing her."

"What a bitch!"

"Sarah!"

"Well, she was!"

"Yes, but she was grieving too. This was her father and she adored him. People act nuts at funerals. And in the hospital. Because they're afraid. So anyway I lost it and started crying like a baby, and she said I could just sit there until I could pull myself together and she left me there. Well, obviously I just cried tears of self-pity for a long time, and after a while I felt considerably better, but I decided to just stay put. I didn't want to go out and see all those relatives I'd embarrassed myself in front of. It was nice and peaceful in the coffee room. So I poured myself a cup and put my feet up."

Sarah was dying to tell her father that this whole story had him acting just like Patrick, but she had a feeling he wouldn't like that. She realized for the first time that maybe the reason he was so hard on Patrick was because they were alike. She made a quick note to that effect in her blank book. Something to think about later.

"Anyway the next part . . . well, you just have to believe me or not . . . I was looking down into my coffee and I glanced up, and there he was."

"Grampa Wills?" Sarah whispered.

He nodded. "Not like a hologram or a cloud of mist or anything. Just a big, solid man standing on the other side of the room, looking at me and shaking his head."

"What did he have on?" Sarah demanded. "A suit? Like the body would have had? Or something else?"

"Something else. He had on khaki pants and a red plaid shirt. It was one of his outfits, all right, but not what that body in the viewing room had on. It was something he wore a lot when I went to his house and we worked in the garden together. It was *my* favorite outfit of his."

Sarah cocked her head. "Doesn't that mean it was all in your mind?"

He paused. He frowned as if carefully retrieving the memory. "It does seem like that. That's what any trained psychiatrist would say. But, Sarah, it didn't feel like that. I can't explain it any better. I don't believe it was my imagination because my imagination isn't that good. If I'd been conjuring him up, he would have come and hugged me and told me I was his favorite person in the family. But he was just standing there shaking his head at me. That's what *he* would have done."

"But your subconscious is smart and clever, right?"

"So they say. Okay, I can't defend it rationally. But it happened to me, and I believe it. I almost feel like sometimes we explain too much away by saying it's all in the mind. It's like that's become a catchall for everything we don't understand. I went to medical school and they tried their best to hammer this stuff out of me, but you know, Sarah, I'm Irish and . . . the Irish see things differently."

"How?"

"Well . . . man is not the center of their universe. He's just a little thing off to the side getting in the way of the important things. In the center there's a whole carnival of unseen things. No one told me this in words when I was little, but I saw it in everything my father and mother did. They respected superstition. They felt like small cogs in a big, powerful magical world."

"But that's just being old-fashioned. That's wrong."

"That's what we're supposed to think."

Sarah had goose bumps. "And you don't?"

"I don't know what I think. But I think my grandfather's ghost came to visit me in the funeral home. I know it did."

Sarah capped her pen and took a deep breath. "I think Shadow's ghost has been visiting me."

He blinked several times. "Shadow? Your cat?"

"Yes. I've been seeing cat shadows. I think she's trying to stay with me and . . . tell me something."

He lowered his eyes for a second, then raised them again. "I know you took her death very hard, Pixie. Harder than I've ever seen a child take the death of a pet. What you need to do is get another cat. Then you won't be imagining—"

"Imagining! Daddy! You just told me this whole story about ghosts being real, and now—"

"Not a cat, honey. I'm talking about people. People have a soul to go on after death. Cats are just . . . animals."

"Animals have a soul!" Sarah said. "Haven't you ever looked in their eyes?"

"I know we love them as if they were people. But they aren't. God made man to be the special one, to have the soul. What would be the point of animals living on after death? They couldn't hunt or do anything they cared about."

"Maybe they reincarnate!"

"What for? Animals don't have faults to correct. It doesn't make sense. The Church teaches us—"

"You're all open-minded if it's something you want to believe in, but you drag in the Church when it's something you don't like."

"Sarah, everyone has a right to believe what they want, but the idea of a cat—"

"You don't know cats like I do! You know you saw your grandfather, and I know what I saw too. And I thought for a minute you might understand but obviously—"

"I understand how you feel, Sarah. You loved that cat like she was a person, and so—"

"Forget it." Sarah got up and stalked away.

"Pixie, I'm sorry! I have to tell you what I honestly think, don't I?"

Sarah didn't answer him.

In the kitchen Cissy was just getting her car keys out of her purse. "Can you stay here a few more minutes?" Sarah asked. "I need to talk to you. It's really important."

Cissy did what she often did. She squinted at Sarah

as if she could "read" her. "Sure," she said. "Let's go out on the porch."

It was a good suggestion. The night air made Sarah feel better immediately. There was a quarter moon casting a faintly greenish light over the yard, sparkling in the wet grass. The jasmine and cypress smell of the neighborhood was stronger than in the daytime. It occurred to Sarah that Florida was a nocturnal part of the world—most of its plant and animal activity took place at night.

Cissy sat in a patio chair, ignoring the dew on her cotton skirt. She beckoned Sarah. "I heard you and your daddy. I didn't mean to, but you were raising your voices. Are you seeing this cat a lot?"

"Yes," Sarah said. "It's scaring me."

Cissy raked her fingers through her hair. "This cat is pressing on me too. She's pressing on my thoughts during the day. She's afraid for someone in this house. It's not you. But it's someone she cares about because of you. I don't know what her problem is, frankly, but this cat is getting on my nerves. When something like this starts to happen, I think the best thing is to try to open up and listen to whatever she wants to say. Let her say it. I think you and I should try to call her in and see if we can do that. Would you be scared?"

Sarah felt cold. She rubbed her arms. In the moonlight Cissy's face was as pale as a statue. Her eyes looked stark and frightening. "You mean we would have something like a séance?"

Cissy waved her hand as if to dismiss something. "Well, I don't like all that terminology. It puts all this stuff in the voodoo realm. The cat wants to talk to you.

We need to get into a quiet place and put ourselves in the right mood and call her and see if she wants to come. Either to me or to you or to both of us. If you want to call that a séance, okay."

"Would you charge me?"

"No, honey. I'd be doing this as your friend. But . . . the only thing is, I don't want your parents to know. I don't think they would like it. They're both scared of your whole thing with the cat and they would think I was using you or playing off your problems. I know that seems dishonest, but when you're . . . different, you learn that being dishonest isn't always such a bad idea."

Sarah wished she had her blank book with her now. She wanted to remember that. "Why would you do this at all? What's it to you?"

Cissy shifted, tucking one foot under herself. "I told you. I can't work in your house without feeling that damn cat pressing on me. I want to resolve it. And . . . well, when you have an ability like mine, there's an obligation that goes with it. Like if your daddy was in some public place and somebody collapsed, he'd feel he had to help because he knows what to do. I see you with this cat following you around and I know how to help. So I've got to."

"Have you done this before? Called people?"

"Called people. Not cats. The whole cat thing is new to me."

"What usually happens? When you call people?"

"Sometimes nothing. Sometimes lots of things. Every case is different. I'm not promising you a thing. But I think we should try."

Sarah's heart was beating hard. "When?"

" 'Where' is a better question. I think we'd better do this at my house so that your parents don't walk in on us and try to burn me at the stake. I just live down in Tamarac. You could get there on your bike."

At Cissy's place there could be all kinds of things rigged up. "No. I want to do it here. The cat is here, so we should do it here. We'll just find a time when nobody's around."

"Okay. Suit yourself."

"In fact what we could do is . . . I could ditch school tomorrow. That's perfect, because Patrick will be off at his picnic and Brian will either go out and act crazy or drink himself into a coma. I'll play sick or something."

Cissy rubbed her palm as if it itched. "I don't know. Now I'm doing something I'm not supposed to in my employer's house and I'm helping you skip school . . . I don't think so. I really love this job."

"Cissy, come on. I'm an honor student. It's the last week of school. We're not doing anything. Please?"

Cissy chewed her lower lip. A minute ago she had looked frightening to Sarah. Now she looked like a little kid on the playground afraid to go down the slide. "You stay home if you want to. And if there's a good opportunity, we'll see what we can do. Okay?"

"Okay."

"I'm really trusting you, Sarah. You could get me in big trouble."

"I'm really trusting you too. You could be fooling me. This could all be like a game to you."

Cissy sighed. "Do I look like I'm having fun? Listen,

get in the house now and make up with your daddy. He's a good man."

"I know."

Cissy got up, ruffled Sarah's hair, and walked off to her rusty Dodge. The dashboard was crammed with stuffed ducks, rabbits, and bears. The bumper sticker said SEE RUBY FALLS. Cissy slid into the driver's seat, adjusted the rearview mirror, which was festooned with prisms and amulets, folded several sticks of gum into her mouth, and roared off.

Sarah watched until she was out of sight, and went back into the house. Her father had put away his checkbook and was now watching a rerun of *Dragnet*. He looked up when Sarah came in. "Honey, I'm sorry. You're entitled to believe whatever you want. I apologize. I'm just worried about you, that's all."

"I know." Sarah casually retrieved her blank book from the table and went to her room. She closed and locked the door and made a final entry:

I'm going to find out the truth no matter what it takes.

Eight

Sarah walked into a hallway with doors, hundreds of doors stretching to infinity. Shadow trotted up and down the hall, the strange, rapid canter she used when an enemy cat or dog was lurking nearby. She would pause at each door, listening for something, then she would look at Sarah urgently, as if Sarah were expected to help her. Dimly, in the background, there were sounds; scuffling, slamming, male voices growling. Sarah could see now that Shadow was trying to decide where the commotion came from.

Sarah floated forward, feeling reluctant because the hallway was heavy with a greenish gloom. The air was stale and chilled. The scuffling sounds echoed up and down the hall, making it difficult to pinpoint direction.

Then Shadow chose a door. It was a distant door, almost lost in the dusk of the deep hallway, but Sarah could still make out the shape of the cat, pawing and scratching, trying to dig under the threshold like a dog.

Sarah moved slowly, too slowly. She wished she

could urge herself forward, but she almost seemed to be attached to a slow-moving dolly. There were bad sounds behind the door now; loud slams and strangled screams. Sarah didn't know if she wanted to see.

Shadow had gone into a frenzy, hurling her dark, compact body against the door. Sarah saw it was one of the bedroom doors in her house; white, brass knob, a little splintered paint at eye level where someone had apparently driven in a nail, then pulled it out.

Sarah looked down at Shadow again and saw that the cat had stopped pacing and was sitting quietly, looking up at Sarah. Behind the door was silence.

"Let's get out of here," Sarah said. The hysterical notes in her voice echoed down the corridor.

The cat just looked at her. *Reproachfully*, Sarah thought.

She turned the knob slowly. Cold wind blew around the edges of the door, into Sarah's face. The cat drew back slightly.

Sarah pulled the door open wide, and the cold wind struck her face hard. When she could open her eyes against it, she saw a bare room. In the middle of the floor lay a shovel, broken in half, surrounded by shards of glass, puddles of water, and a handful of wilting marigolds. Somewhere far in the distance she heard a young man sobbing.

Shadow walked into the room slowly, circled the shovel, then rubbed her head against the splintered handle. Before Sarah could follow her, the wind slammed the door shut.

Sarah screamed herself awake.

She was back in her own bedroom, safe for the moment. She savored the details of the waking world, the white windowpanes framing the sunlit lawn. It was just after sunrise. Tuesday. Patrick's picnic day. Séance-with-the-cat day. Not a moment too soon. Sarah picked up the blank book on her night table, intending to write down the dream, then changed her mind. She didn't want to remember it all that much. Maybe her father was right. Maybe she needed to get another cat and stop dwelling on Shadow's death.

Sarah got up and made the bed hurriedly, anxious to get away from that location. She washed her face, brushed her hair, and tied on her flowered kimono. Then she slapped herself in the face several times to simulate a feverish flush. She looked in the mirror and thought the effect was good.

In the kitchen Cissy was cooking breakfast for Patrick and Brian, who faced each other across the kitchen table. The topic of discussion this morning appeared to be Patrick's car.

"I don't want you ever touching it," Patrick said.

"Blow off," Brian muttered, pretending to read the paper. "Dad said I could have it, and anyway it was *my* car before it was your car."

"It's mine now," Patrick said. "And you have to ask me, not Dad, when you want it."

"Eat shit and die," Brian said mildly. "If she's picking you up, then you don't need the car for the whole goddamn day. And I do."

"What do you need it for?" Patrick asked. "I don't want you driving around drunk in it."

Brian repositioned the newspaper to block Patrick out. "I'm going to pick up a bunch of incontinent old men and drive them around. Then I'll take a shortcut through a swamp and visit a leper colony."

Patrick sat back, frustrated for a moment. Then he smiled. "Hey, go ahead. Knock yourself out. I'm a happy man. All I really care about is seeing what Karen has in her picnic basket." For good measure he reached across the table and thwacked Brian's newspaper. The noise startled everyone.

Brian jumped to his feet. "You'd better quit it, you little mosquito, or I'll swat you!" He brandished the paper menacingly.

"Here now!" said Cissy from the stove.

"Good morning!" Sarah said loudly. Then she leaned against the doorframe and tried to look weak.

"Good morning, Sarah." Cissy said, frowning. "Are you all right?"

"I feel a little funny." Sarah wobbled to the table and sat down. "Where's Mom? Did she leave for work yet?"

"No, she's still getting dressed." Cissy gave Sarah a significant look. "She's going in late because she worked late last night. You want some French toast?"

Damn! Sarah thought. French toast was her favorite. She looked at her brothers' plates. Cissy made it golden and puffy, frosted with powdered sugar. "No." Sarah sighed. "I couldn't eat a thing." She sat down next to Patrick and put her head in her hands.

"I want your opinion," Patrick said. "Do you think Dad should tell Brian he's free to use my car?"

"Give it a rest, Trick," Sarah said, sipping her orange juice. "Can't you see I'm ill?"

He squinted at her. "You look like somebody took a pop at you!"

Luckily the phone rang. "I'll get it!" Patrick exploded from his chair.

"Jeez God!" Brian said.

Patrick assumed a strange, sexy voice. "Hello? Oh, hi, Karen." He smiled sweetly at Brian. "Yeah. Oh, sure. Now is not too early. Yeah, we can—" He broke off and giggled at something she said.

"I am going to put an incontinent old man in his car," Brian muttered.

Sarah sat back in her chair and tried to think feverish thoughts. Patrick had said yoga experts could elevate their temperature and blood pressure at will.

Patrick's voice had gotten low. "Sure. Sure. Yeah, I'd like that a lot. Me too. Okay. Good-bye." He sauntered back to the table. "Here," he said, passing his plate to Brian. "I can't eat breakfast. Karen can't wait to pick me up. She'll be over here in a few minutes."

"You idiot!" Brian said, although he accepted the plate. "Don't you have any pride? Don't you see what she's trying to do?"

"Date human beings instead of animals?"

Sarah sat up and took a slow, theatrical sip of juice, then sank back again. She actually was beginning to feel funny.

Brian shoved his paper aside. "Patrick, no kidding. She's just using you to put on a show for me. Deep down you know that. I know you're desperate, but you don't have to act like a complete doormat."

"I appreciate your concern," Patrick said. "It's touching."

"You . . ."

Sarah felt a cool hand on her forehead. "Where does it hurt?" Cissy asked.

"All over," Sarah said. "Achy, feverish."

"Want me to take your temperature?"

"Yeah, thanks. The thermometer is in the bathroom closet across from the boys' room."

"It's my room!" Patrick said.

Cissy put her hands on her hips. "I realize I just work here and I'm not much older than you are, but I'm telling you, if I hear one more silly thing like that out of either one of you, I am going to scream. Your sister is sick and the two of you are going right on with your old stupid argument. You're supposed to be so smart, but I really don't see the evidence of it! Especially you, Patrick. You got what you want, you're going out with his girlfriend, so why don't you be a little gracious? I swear to God, if you were my boy and I was your mama, I'd put you right across my knee, seventeen years old or not, and spank you till you couldn't sit down!" She turned on her heel and marched out.

Patrick looked stunned. "What did I do?" he asked.

Sarah was about to tell him, but the doorbell rang.

"I guess that's Karen," Patrick said softly. "I'll go let her in." He left, looking dazed.

"About time somebody told him off." Brian smirked.

"You're just as bad," Sarah said.

He picked up the paper again.

Karen bounced into the kitchen, looking radiant in her pink playsuit. "Hi, everybody!" she said. Patrick followed her in, still looking a little out of it.

"Hurry up and go if you're going," Brian said.

Karen gave him a patronizing smile. Then she turned to Sarah. "I heard you weren't feeling well."

"It's nothing," Sarah said.

"Aww." Karen came over and felt Sarah's forehead, in the process bending over with her back to Brian. He looked out the window in disgust.

"It's just a little bug or something," Sarah said, pulling back.

Cissy returned with the thermometer. Patrick stepped briskly aside to let her pass. " 'Scuze me," Cissy said, pushing Karen gently out of the way. She put the thermometer in Sarah's mouth, then straightened up and looked at Karen with narrowed eyes. "How're you doin' today?" she asked in a voice that was definitely not friendly.

Karen took a step back. "Fine." She turned to Patrick. "Are you ready to go?"

He was still looking at Cissy, as if he wanted something. "Yeah. I just have to go put my shoes on."

Karen walked over to him. "I'll be waiting in the car," she said in a low voice. She leaned in and gave him a kiss, putting her arms around his waist as if to hold him there. Patrick began to blush, but put his arms around Karen and kissed back. Sarah's thermometer beeped.

Karen finally let go. "I'll be waiting," she said. She slung her purse over her shoulder and strolled out, long legs flashing, tight shorts rolling.

Patrick sat down at the table as if his legs were giving away. "Wow!" he said. He picked up a napkin and fanned himself.

Cissy took the thermometer out of Sarah's mouth and read it. "You've got a degree of temperature. Maybe you should stay home."

"Better take Patrick's temperature too." Sarah giggled.

He grinned at her. "Be quiet!"

She leaned toward him confidentially. "Were you using your tongue?"

The whole kitchen table went over with a crash.

Sarah felt hot coffee splash up into her face and maple syrup trickle over her hands.

Everyone moved at once. Patrick screamed and covered his eyes. Sarah stood up, which caused the table somehow to crash again in a slide of broken glasses and dishes. Brian, who had apparently caused the catastrophe, was standing over the wreckage, red-faced with rage, panting and looking at Patrick as if he wanted to do something else. Still half blinded, Sarah saw Cissy run first toward Brian as if to censure him, then change direction and go to Patrick, who had obviously taken hot coffee, or something worse, in the eye.

"It's not glass, is it?" she asked, leaning over him anxiously.

He shook his head.

"Is it coffee? Here, come here and let me rinse it out."

She helped him stand, walked him to the sink, and put his head under the faucet. Then she turned, puffing with anger, to Brian, who was beginning to look a bit astonished at the spectacular mess on the floor. "You're a piece of work, aren't you, mister?" Cissy said angrily.

"What if you'd really hurt him? Or your sister? Don't you ever think? Any of you?" She shut off the water and straightened Patrick up, looking into his face. "Is it okay, sweetheart? Are your eyes okay?"

He nodded, dripping all over her. He was soaked. He stepped back from Cissy and tried to fluff his drenched hair. Then he turned to Brian with an expression Sarah didn't like.

Sarah was paralyzed by mixed emotions. Foremost in her mind was that there was a tremendous mess here and their mother was lurking somewhere in the house. Also, Sarah was angry at being included in Cissy's immaturity lectures, which she felt applied only to her brothers. But the main thing to worry about was that neither Brian nor Patrick seemed finished with this fight. They just stood watching each other like cowboys at high noon, waiting for a signal to draw.

"You piece of shit," Patrick snarled. "If you had hurt Sarah with your cute little thing here, I'd cut out your heart and make you eat it."

"I want you to leave Karen alone," Brian said quietly. "Playtime is over, and I've had enough of this crap. I'm real serious about this. If you keep this up, I'm gonna do something to you a whole lot worse than this."

"You guys!" Sarah said, finally finding her voice.

Patrick pushed back a handful of wet hair. "I'm not afraid of you," he replied quietly.

"You should be."

They both continued to glare. Their hatred was like some kind of volatile gas filling up the room. A wrong move by anyone and it would explode.

"Leave her alone," Brian said. "I mean it."

Patrick took a deep breath. "No. I like her. And she deserves someone better than you."

"Stop it, both of you!" Cissy said. "I mean it. Right now."

Brian began to move. Holding Patrick's eyes, he walked around the wreckage of the table, crunching a piece of glass underfoot.

"No!" Sarah shrieked. "Leave him alone!"

"I'm not afraid of him!" Patrick shouted, although his eyes wavered a little.

"Don't do something you're going to be sorry for!" Cissy warned, but there was obviously nothing she could do. The top of her head didn't come to the middle of Brian's chest. Sarah's stomach began to twist with helpless fear. She remembered other beatings Brian had given Patrick over the years. Some of them had been terrible. And this one would be worse than any of them.

"No!" Sarah said, blocking Brian with her body.

"Get out of my way," he said. "Now!"

Mrs. Shaheen appeared in the doorway. Everyone froze. Her eyes went wide, taking in the scene, then narrowed to pinpoints of rage. "What in the name of God is going on here?" she shouted.

"The boys were arguing, and there was a little accident," Cissy said. "They're going to clean it up right now."

"You're darn right they are!" Mrs. Shaheen cried. "Brian Shaheen, what in the *devil* is the matter with you?"

"He . . ." he began, pointing at Patrick.

"I don't want to hear it. You go get a bucket and a

mop right now. Patrick, get the trash can and pick up all this broken stuff."

"Karen's waiting for me in the car," he said.

"Karen can wait. Do it. Sarah, you're in your bare feet. Go put some shoes on before you cut yourself." She turned to Cissy. "How could you let something like this happen?"

Cissy lifted her chin. "I'm not being paid to be a baby-sitter, Mrs. Shaheen, and these are not little kids. If you think I'm going to get between two boys this size—"

"Which one of them did this to the table?"

Cissy lowered her eyes. "I think Brian stood up too suddenly."

"Well, that figures." She turned her wrath back to Brian. "Do I have to keep you in a playpen at age nineteen?"

Brian took a deep, angry breath. "No, but he—"

"Get the mop, Brian!"

"He—"

"Get it now."

Brian slunk away. Patrick followed him.

Mrs. Shaheen turned to Sarah. "Why are you still here? What did I tell you to do?"

"Get shoes," Sarah said.

"Then get shoes. Now! Go!"

Sarah edged carefully past her mother and bolted. Behind her she heard Mrs. Shaheen launching one of her truly fine tirades. "Don't think you two aren't going to have to pay for every single broken thing here! Just *wait* until your father finds out about this. You are so lucky he wasn't here when this happened. He'd take both of you macho characters and . . ."

Sarah noticed she was having trouble walking down the hall and realized her legs were shaking. She stopped and leaned against the wall for a second, trying to recover. That had been too close. Brian had always had a temper, but he had never done anything this dramatic before. And Patrick had never had such a good way of baiting him before. If Mrs. Shaheen hadn't walked in when she did . . . Sarah closed her eyes, listening to the faint sounds in the kitchen; her mother still railing and making speeches, both boys trying to plead their cause, the creak and thud of the table being righted. It was really irritating how this whole mess had upstaged Sarah's attempts to play sick. She'd have to wait for this fervor to die down and start all over again.

With a few deep breaths, she was able to get her shaking under control. Then she opened her eyes and stared at what was in front of her. It was the door to Brian and Patrick's room. Like all the bedroom doors in the house it was white with a brass knob. But at eye level there was an area of chipped paint, as if someone had driven in a nail and drawn it back out. Her brothers' door was the door from her dreams.

Nine

On *Another Life*, Dr. Craig DuCamp was slipping into bed with his brother's wife, Brook. Brook was wearing a black lace teddy and diamond earrings. Sarah wondered if real women wore their earrings when they went to bed with men. Did men like that? She also wondered why the men went to bed naked but the women wore nightgowns. Was that common? Her own parents kept the bedroom door locked, so there was no telling what went on in there. Of course you couldn't see the naked men in soap operas, all you saw was their shoulders, but the men always had bare shoulders and the women, even right after sex, had straps. Sarah decided to ask her mother when she came in with the next round of scary food. It would be a kind of revenge.

She didn't have long to wait. Just as Dr. DuCamp's brother, Lane, burst into the room with a Colt .45, Mrs. Shaheen wheeled into the living room carrying a steaming bowl of something beige. "You're going to love this," she commanded.

Sarah sniffed. It smelled like the back door of a dry-cleaning shop. "What is it?"

"Hot Krunch Nuggets! I made it in the microwave. And of course I added a little something special."

That was where things usually went wrong with Mrs. Shaheen's cooking. Those little special things she added. You either have a knack for adding little things or you don't.

Sarah took the bowl and stared at it. The cereal had sort of melted and re-fused into something like textured vinyl. "Tell me the extra thing you put in, Mom," Sarah said.

"Taste it first."

"Uh-uh. No way."

"Okay, if you're going to be like that. Well, the recipe says to add milk and microwave it. But I know how much you like apricot nectar. . . ."

"Oh, barf, Mom!"

"Taste it, sweetie. I had some in the kitchen, and it was fabulous!"

"You did not!"

Mrs. Shaheen's eyes narrowed. "Don't call your mother a liar, dear. Now eat."

"I think I'm feeling nauseated again."

"You get nauseated every time I bring you food!"

"Well, you know, it's the smell and all. How about some cookies or something?"

"What kind of a mother would feed a sick child cookies?"

The mother of my fantasies, Sarah thought. The whole day had been a disaster. The plan had been for Sarah to play sick so that she and Cissy could conduct their séance. After they'd cleaned up the breakfast nook, it had looked as if things would go well. Patrick went off on his picnic. Brian, after enduring a long lecture from his mother, had taken off in Patrick's car. But Sarah hadn't reckoned with the power of maternal instinct. Mrs. Shaheen decided to work on her column at home and fax it in to the paper so that she could prepare these poisonous snacks for her baby girl. If this kept up till Patrick came home, the whole game would be up, unless Sarah could buy his silence. But there was no way Mrs. Shaheen was going anywhere. She hadn't had a sick child to fuss over in years and she was obviously enjoying herself. Cissy, who probably would have made a wonderful chicken noodle soup, had been banished to reorganize the linen cupboards while Mrs. Shaheen set up her evil laboratory in the kitchen.

So there was nothing left for Sarah but revenge. She blew on the congealed nightmare in her hands and said sweetly, "Can I ask you a few questions about sex?"

Mrs. Shaheen reddened. She hated to talk about sex. Patrick held the theory that she hated sex, period. But that wasn't clearly established. Anyway, as an enlightened, well-educated woman of the nineties, she had informed her children that she wanted them to have free, frank discussions with her about any aspect of sexuality anytime they wanted to. So whenever any of them got really pissed off, they invented embarrassing questions for her and laughed silently as she struggled with her answers. Mrs. Shaheen sat on the edge of the couch and took Sarah's hand. "What is it, dear?" she asked apprehensively.

"What do you and Daddy wear to bed when you're going to have sex?"

"What?"

"The people in the soap operas always do the same thing. The lady wears a nightgown and the man doesn't wear anything."

Mrs. Shaheen whirled to confront the television screen. "Are they showing naked men on that monstrosity of a program?"

"No, they don't show it," Sarah said impatiently. "But you can tell." She gave her Krunch Nuggets an experimental tap with her spoon. It seemed to have formed a hardened crust. Sarah made a mental note that this might work as a science project on igneous rocks. "So is that the way it really is? Don't men like to look at naked women?"

Mrs. Shaheen grimaced. "I thought you were watching that zebra program on the Discovery channel."

"It's over. There's nothing on in the afternoon but soaps."

Mrs. Shaheen sighed. "It's just a television thing, honey. They probably can't show women with bare shoulders."

"So when you have sex, everyone is completely naked?"

Mrs. Shaheen closed her eyes as if to shut out a horrible vision. "Generally speaking."

"Would you wear makeup and earrings like those women on TV?"

"Certainly not. That would be very tarty. And not too practical either. You don't want to smear makeup all over your clean sheets, do you?"

"Do you guys leave the lights on?"

"Sarah, I'd prefer if you ask general questions, not specifics about your father and me."

Sarah glanced around her mother at the TV. There was a Hanes underwear commercial on now. A famous baseball star wearing bright blue briefs was jumping up and down on a sofa. Sarah watched with interest. "Do most people do it with the lights on or off?"

"It probably depends on how attractive the people are. What are you looking at now?" Mrs. Shaheen turned around. "Good heavens! What next?"

"Probably the douche commercial. They run that thing about every twenty seconds."

"You should have seen what TV was like when I was your age. We never even saw men in sports clothes. When Ward Cleaver came home from work, he just took off his suit jacket and put on a nice cardigan sweater. He left on his shirt and tie and everything."

Mrs. Shaheen often referred to the Cleaver family, whom Sarah had seen several times in syndication. They were unusually neat and clean people, but hardly anything ever happened to them. They could do a whole show on one of their sons getting lost in a department store. But Sarah's parents always watched the show with a kind of eerie fascination. Sarah couldn't tell if they were thrilled or horrified by the way things used to be.

Mrs. Shaheen turned away from the Hanes commercial, pursing her mouth. Then she looked down at Sarah. "You aren't eating."

Sarah tapped her spoon against the stuff. "I can't get into it."

Mrs. Shaheen took the bowl and looked at it suspiciously. "How do you like that? They put a recipe on the cereal box that doesn't even work. I have a good mind to put this in a column."

"Don't you have to go *finish* your column?" Sarah said hopefully. In a minute *The Rich and the Ravishing* would be on. They had the hottest guys.

"It's all done. I wrote it during your last nap. As a matter of fact you inspired it. I wrote about the special feelings a mother has when she's home taking care of children. And I thought of a lot of cute things that happened when you kids were sick over the years."

Sarah felt a chill. Images of terror danced in her mind. "You didn't mention that family reunion where I sat on the wasp, did you?"

Her mother smiled. "That got a whole paragraph. If you could have seen yourself hopping up and down, howling like a banshee."

Sarah wondered if she could stay home the rest of the week. The kids at school wouldn't be kind about this.

"You've got to eat something, sweetheart. You haven't eaten all day. Can't I tempt you with anything?"

It was two o'clock. The situation was desperate. It was now or never. Sarah thought quickly. "Do you know what sounds really good? Cherry vanilla ice cream."

"Cherry vanilla! We haven't had that in years. What made you think of that?"

The fact that I haven't seen it in any of the stores for five years. "I don't know. Maybe talking about old family

reunions. I went through a time when I really loved it."
This was a bald-faced lie.

"Really? Well, I guess I could run out and get some.
Would you be okay alone with Cissy?"

"Oh, sure."

"All right. Anything else?"

*An insurance policy. In case you have dumb luck and find
cherry vanilla ice cream on the first try.* "Strawberry Newtons."

Her mother laughed. "That's like Fig Newtons?"

"Yeah. Only with strawberries."

Her mother ruffled Sarah's hair. "You're a strange
child. All right, I'll be back as soon as I can."

"Here, take this." Sarah offered her the bowl of
Krunch Nuggets, which was growing mysteriously heavy
as further chemical interactions took place.

Mrs. Shaheen fussed around for several more minutes, giving Cissy a long series of improbable instruc-
tions, but finally she left. Sarah counted to fifteen—
sometimes Mrs. Shaheen forgot her wallet—then clicked
off the TV set.

"Cissy?" she called.

No answer.

Feeling pleasantly spooky already, Sarah rolled off
the couch, stretched, and went exploring. She found
Cissy kneeling in the hallway, surrounded by piles of
guest towels and pillowcases. Cissy looked up and
grinned. "Is the coast clear?" she asked.

"Yes." Sarah's hands twined and untwined.

Cissy drew her blond eyebrows down in mock stern-
ness. "Are you sure you want to do this, Sarah? Because
you look a little nervous."

Sarah hugged herself. "Nervous! Are you kidding? I'm dying to do this. I think this is going to be great."

Cissy continued to stare. Her eyes were as pale as Coke-bottle glass, the pupils slightly enlarged. Sarah had the feeling, as she had had several times before, that she was being scanned or "read" in some way. "Something might happen," Cissy said. She said it in a monotone, but it sent huge, slow shivers through Sarah.

"I know," Sarah said in the steadiest voice she could manage.

Cissy still looked at her a minute longer, then got up as fluidly and gracefully as a ballet dancer, gathering stacks of pastel linens and arranging them in the closet. "Let's use your room," she said over her shoulder.

Sarah didn't move. She just watched the fluid sway of Cissy's back. *This person is really a complete stranger to me*, Sarah thought. She remembered some older girls at a day camp once who had talked her into skinny-dipping with them. Then they had stolen her clothes. This could be the same kind of thing.

Still, Sarah knew she had to go through with it. Mostly because she needed to understand all the weird things that had been happening to her. If Cissy was wrong or lying, it might mean Sarah was crazy.

Cissy went ahead of Sarah into her room and sat cross-legged in the middle of Sarah's bed. She closed her eyes and frowned. "Close the verticals," she muttered.

Her tone made Sarah obey without question. The room dissolved into shadows.

"Now, sit . . ." Cissy spoke haltingly. "Sit down here in front of me." She continued to keep her eyes closed. Sarah had the definite impression Cissy was listening to something else as she spoke. She sounded just like an anchorwoman getting an urgent message from the floor director over her earphones.

Cissy took several very deep breaths. They sounded loud and eerie in the silence. *Darth Vader*, Sarah thought. She pulled her knees up to her chest and hugged them.

"It's good," Cissy said. "It's a good . . ."

Sarah wanted to scream "What? What's going on?" but she kept her silence.

Cissy opened her eyes suddenly. "Call your cat," she said.

Sarah's heart began to pound. "What?" she whispered.

Cissy was almost panting. She closed her eyes and opened them again. "Call your cat! Now!"

Sarah could hardly breathe. She felt as if some kind of cold, heavy mist were filling the room. In her mind she *saw* the mist, gray-green, wispy, icy cold. "I—"

"She's here! Don't fight this! Call her!"

"Shadow?" Sarah's voice was a terrified squeak.

The mist in Sarah's mind began to pitch and roll. She lost track of her surroundings, as if she were falling into a dream, only backward. Instead of closing her eyes and seeing the dream in her mind, she felt that the image from her mind had come outside and filled the room.

Fingers of green fog caressed her face. It was warmer now, inviting. She could hardly see through it, but she had a feeling for the landscape in back of it. She was in a jungle, a tangle of black vines and ropy roots. There was a fascinating mixture of smells. Musk? Spring water? The beach? Animals seemed to be prowling, although she didn't see their outlines. She felt their movements. Cat movements. "Where am I?" Sarah bleated.

Cissy's voice came clear and steady, although Cissy was nowhere around. "I don't know, but I see it too. It's all right. You're still safe in your bedroom. But call her again. Call the cat."

"Shadow?" Sarah called faintly. "Are you here?"

She could now hear them in the depths of the musky jungle, trills and purrs and meows, leaves rustling under creeping feet. It was a warm, dark, foggy cat jungle.

Sarah's voice cracked with emotion. "Shadow? Is this your . . . heaven?"

Then she saw what must have been there all along. A tree branch only a few feet away with moss and vines trailing from its leafless branch. On the branch sat Shadow, not quite as she looked at the end of her life. It was Shadow in her prime, full, fat, glossy. Shadow had been staring right down at her, and when Sarah finally saw her, she switched her tail.

"Shadow," Sarah said very softly. She didn't feel like crying. Everything suddenly felt calm and right and perfectly normal. There was even some sunlight now, piercing the fog in vertical shafts, illuminating a beautiful, deep forest carpeted with moss. It seemed to go on forever. There were cats everywhere, dozing, licking, stalking, and pouncing at invisible things. Not just house cats either. Lions and leopards and, not far away, a huge white tiger. No cubs or kittens. No old or sick or lame. None of them except Shadow looked at Sarah or paid her the slightest attention.

Sarah realized this was all completely fantastic, but

she didn't feel frightened or weird. It was just like a dream, where weird things seem perfectly normal. She felt that somehow Shadow was doing something to her to keep her calm. Shadow's eyes were shining down at Sarah's with deep love. A look Sarah had often seen before. "Where is this?" she asked.

The answer was in her mind, but it came from outside. *Between.*

"Are you happy here?"

I won't stay.

"Why?"

You.

"I don't understand."

Watch.

Sarah was struck by a sudden gust of wind that shattered her tranquillity. She felt almost enraged at being disturbed in that beautiful place. The wind blinded her. It was so white. It was like the clouds. It was like flying through clouds in an airplane. It was beautiful, but Sarah felt impatient. She couldn't see Shadow. She couldn't see where she was going. She was moving fast, hurtling through this opaque wind, and then a series of images detonated like bursts of fireworks in front of her. A sudden light. A woman's black dress being trampled. A huge explosion of ice or glass. A half-naked woman sprinting across a moonlit lawn. Male bodies charging or flying. Panic. A plunge into darkness, shadows. The smell of sweat and alcohol. Pain. A telephone high in the sky. Male grunting, gasping. Sarah felt a terrible sense of panic, as if a ravine had opened at her feet . . . then a growl, the animal growling, screaming, the sound of an unearthly animal scream and pain, pain, blood and claws and . . .

Cissy sat in front of her in the silent, dark room, her hands up to her mouth as if to hold in a scream, her eyes wide with fear. "Is it over, Sarah?" she asked in a small voice.

Sarah was drenched in sweat, breathing in racking gasps, feeling as if all her molecules had been scattered and had to regather before she could speak. "What was all that?" she cried. "What happened?"

Cissy bit her lower lip. "You're a lot more talented than I thought," she said.

Cissy placed a cup of tea in Sarah's shaking hands. "How do you feel now?" she asked.

Sarah nodded slightly to indicate she felt better. More than anything, she felt distracted. She wanted to remember everything she'd seen.

Cissy sat on the bed. "Let me give you some friendly advice, Sarah. Don't tell anyone about this. Ever. Just people like me who'll understand. You've got a huge gift. If you'd focus it, there's no telling what you could see."

"You think those were . . . visions?" Sarah said softly. The tea had a comforting effect. Sarah was afraid to ask what kind it was.

Cissy nodded. "Your cat was trying to show you something."

"But I don't understand what she was showing me. It was horrible."

"That's the way it is sometimes."

"Did you see everything I saw?"

"I saw things flying around. Bodies. Glass. A woman running across a yard. People bleeding and getting cut up. But it was very confusing."

Sarah reached out impulsively and took Cissy's hand. It was almost the same size as hers. "If you hadn't seen it, too, I'd think I was crazy."

"You're not crazy, Sarah. This happens to certain people all the time. But listen to what I said. Don't tell anybody who might not understand. You're very special. Special people have to be careful."

"I guess you would know."

"I know."

Sarah put her tea down. She pushed her hair back with a shaky hand. "Cissy . . . there's a whole lot more to the world than any of us knows, isn't there?"

Cissy smiled. "Now you're catching on," she said.

Ten

After the séance Sarah dreamed of Shadow almost every night; different variations of the same themes. Danger, violence, the cat leading her to various doors, showing her things behind them. Sometimes, lately, they were sex dreams. The cat would urge her toward a door and she'd open it and see people with no clothes on, rushing to cover themselves. Then she'd feel angry with Shadow for embarrassing her. "Is this what you wanted me to see?" she shouted in one dream, her voice reverberating down a long hallway that was paved with some kind of hammered bronze. The next morning Sarah realized the hallway was made out of the same material she'd seen at her grandfather's funeral. Coffin metal.

She bought a book on ESP. It gave her exercises to do, such as turning over playing cards and guessing which suits would come up or trying to anticipate traffic lights when riding in the car. Sometimes she thought she did very well, other times she did miserably. Cissy said a lot of that was influenced by thinking and having emotions. She said only when you were clear and alert could you really funnel impressions. If you worried about the outcome of a test, you'd fail. Cissy said that was why it was difficult to predict anything for yourself or your loved ones. "You listen to your own worries and hopes instead of the message."

Sometimes Sarah thought the whole thing was a crock of shit.

Meanwhile they seemed to be having the hottest summer on record. Usually, in Florida, you could count on an afternoon thunderstorm to break things up, but this year it was just hot and humid, humid and hot. Julian went to Orlando with his parents for a week, making it hot, humid, and dull. Sarah really didn't have any other close friends, believing in quality over quantity. So there was nothing to do but hang around the house in her bikini, painting her fingernails and toenails different colors while she read endless back issues of *Seventeen* and *Sassy*.

The only real events in the day were the quarrels between her brothers. They wanted to fight over Karen, but Brian was too cool to act like he cared, so instead they fought over the use of Patrick's car.

"Give me the keys, Trish," Brian would say, usually adding some physical insult to the request, such as knocking Patrick's feet off the coffee table or jerking a Walkman out of his ears.

Patrick would usually respond with his favorite quote: "Eat shit and die." Then they'd once again go over the pros and cons of their rights and responsibilities, both of them speaking for the opinions of their father, who was never there.

"Shut up, you guys," Sarah said one afternoon, when the heat had given her a headache. "Get a new program. I'm tired of this rerun."

Brian, who was shirtless and threatening-looking, folded his arms. He was standing over Patrick, who pretended to be absorbed in a talk show. "Are you going out tonight, Patrick?" he asked in a tone of mock forbearance.

"Don't know yet." Patrick made a hushing gesture with his hand. Then he looked up at Brian with an almost puckish smile. "I have to call my girl."

Brian closed his eyes and took a deep breath. "I'm trying to be reasonable with you," he said.

"It's obviously taking its toll." Patrick grinned.

"Dad said he wanted you to share the car with me."

"You should have driven down here and then you'd have your own car."

"You're just mad because he paid for my plane ticket. You've been mad about that ever since I came."

"I'm mad because I don't want you doing God knows what in my clean car. What if you get drunk and smash it up? Whose insurance goes up? Mine. No, I'm sorry. I have to use my discretion."

Sarah tuned out for a while, since this part of the argument always went the same. She focused on *Oprah* instead. The topic was women who had attempted to murder their husbands. It was the most cheerful-looking panel Sarah had ever seen on the show.

"I tried to poison the bastard," said a slim redhead. "But it didn't work. He didn't even get sick!"

The audience laughed appreciatively. Sarah wondered what was wrong with her that she didn't find this funny.

She turned back to her brothers. With his arms folded Brian looked more muscular than usual. There was a faint sheen of sweat on his back. Patrick, who never seemed to perspire, had picked up the cordless phone and was apparently calling Karen.

"Hi," he said coyly. "Wha'cha doing?"

"Shit," said Brian, sitting down on the rug.

"Yeah," Patrick said. "Yeah, I am. That's why I called. Do you want to do something tonight?"

"Little shit," Brian murmured.

"After I hit him three times with the stupid thing, he finally stayed down," said a woman on television. "But I thought, hey, at least this is one way to keep him home at night."

Sarah turned off the TV.

"Shorts. Plaid shorts. What have *you* got on?" Patrick asked. He was flushed.

"Oh, for Christ's sake!" Brian exploded.

"Yeah? Well, I don't have to answer that." Patrick giggled. "Maybe you can find out tonight. You want to go to the drive-in with me?"

"You went there last night," Brian said.

Patrick muffled the receiver. "We *like* to go there." He smiled.

Brian rolled his eyes.

"Yeah, well, I need to know. Brian wants the car. Who knows? Probably a peep show or something. Wherever lonely guys go—"

"Give me that phone!" Brian exploded, dragging the

receiver out of Patrick's hand. "Hey!" he shouted at Karen. "When are you going to cut this shit out and act normal again? No! I will not! I want you to answer me! Don't you even feel guilty about what you're doing to him? He's stupid, you know. He's buying this whole routine."

"Give me back the phone, Brian," Patrick said calmly.

"You know, when you decide to cut out this little game, it may be too late! I may just decide . . . oh, shit, what's the use? Here." He gave the phone back to Patrick and stalked out of the room. Sarah heard him open the refrigerator.

"Now is fine," Patrick said. "I just have to go put on a shirt. No, we can eat someplace first. Sure, I know. No, I'm used to it. Don't worry. Yeah." He grinned at the phone. "I know you do. I'll see you soon. 'Bye." He cradled the receiver tenderly, as if it had feelings.

"Do you really like her?" Sarah asked.

He was already on his way to his room to change. He stopped on one foot, like a stork, as if Sarah had asked an amazing question. "Of course I do!"

"Are you sure?"

"Look at her! What's not to like?"

"Nothing, nothing, it's just that I would think you'd go for a more intellectual type."

He slowly lowered his foot to the carpet. "Well," he said with a little half laugh. "*You* know, Pixie. You like different girls for different reasons. I mean . . . look at her."

"Yeah, I know," Sarah said. She turned the TV back on.

But Patrick seemed discontented now. "We've been talking a lot," he said. "Karen and me. Brian really treated her badly. She appreciates someone being nice to her."

"Sure, I can see that." The back door slammed. Brian had gone out into the yard with whatever he took from the refrigerator.

"You act like there's something else you want to say," Patrick insisted.

"No." Sarah looked up. "There isn't."

"Like you think something's going to go wrong. Like you think something bad's going to happen."

That was exactly it. "I'm not psychic," Sarah said, feeling she was telling a lie.

"No," he said forcefully. "You're not." He went off down the hall.

Sarah got up immediately and went out to the back-yard. Brian was in his favorite deck chair, tipping up a chilled bottle of Chablis, staring at the sun going down over the hibiscus hedge. Sarah heard a voice in her head saying, *Bad, bad.* She approached with caution, sitting in the chair next to his, but watching him in case he ordered her to leave. "Don't you want a glass?" she asked, trying for a laugh.

He just shook his head. *Bad, bad.* Sarah realized she was receiving. She sat very still and realized she could feel Brian's feelings pushing down on the middle of her chest. His feelings were a big, heavy weight that covered the whole yard and pushed down on everything. She could feel the inside of his mind. Despair. It was despair, much worse than she ever would have guessed. She knew the feeling.

The veterinarian's office. The warring smells of animal functions and antiseptics. Holding Shadow in her arms. Once a weighty bundle, the cat was like an armload of feathers now. Sarah wished she could put her down, but the steel examining table always looked so cold.

Dr. Metzger's face. His round blue eyes. So horribly, disgustingly kind. You couldn't even get angry or shout, because he was feeling the pain too. "With an animal, quality of life is even more important than with a human," he was saying. "Humans have a mental life, but to an animal his physical body is everything. When they can't eat, when they can't run and play, they've lost their reason to be."

Sarah felt all her little corners of hope going out. The hope that just by discovering the right food they could make Shadow want to eat again. The hope that suddenly Dr. Metzger would have a flash of insight and remember a miracle drug that kept animals from aging. The hope that if she made the right promises to God, Sarah would be spared this terrible, terrible impending event.

"I can put her here in the hospital, feed her intravenously, and she'll stay alive for several more months. But she'll keep wasting away. Keep feeling worse and worse every day until the end. Or you can take her home and give her a weekend full of love, let her spend her last time on earth with you, and then you can bring her in on Monday and do the responsible thing."

The grieving really started then, that moment, when all the hope was extinguished. As soon as Sarah knew Shadow was going to die, she was the same as dead. It was a heavy, pushing-down feeling right in the middle of the chest. It lasted for four full months after Shadow died, making it necessary for Sarah to sigh and take sudden, deep breaths just to get enough oxygen. The whole world was slow, dark, and heavy. Sometimes it was hard to see.

Brian was feeling that way right now. Sarah was almost afraid to speak to him, to break in on such sadness. For a few minutes she just sat and felt it with him. It was a shock. She'd always thought of him as completely insensitive.

The sun flared as it fell, casting back a fiery light on Brian's face. He tilted the bottle again. The wine splashed up and back. Both he and the bottle were sweating freely.

Sarah sensed something and looked back toward the house. Patrick stood at the edge of the yard, his clean white shirt glowing like radium in the dim light. "Goodbye, Sarah," he said uncertainly.

" 'Bye," she said faintly.

He hesitated a minute longer as if he wanted more, then disappeared. The car revved up and drove away. Brian took another drink. Slosh-up, slosh-down. The sky at the zenith had begun to darken, dramatizing the fiery streaks on the horizon.

Sarah decided to take a chance. "If you really love Karen, you ought to try harder to get her back."

"S'not that," he said, taking a swig with his eyes closed. "It's him, you know? It's him. I'm so fucking sick of him, I could die."

Sarah believed him. "Why? What has he ever done to you? I mean, up until now?"

"It's . . . no . . . it's more complicated than that. Wait." He took another long pull at the bottle. It was more than half gone. Sarah realized Brian was so drunk, he would actually open up to her. "He's . . . why is he there, Sarah? Why's he even have to be there? I'm good enough. It coulda been just me and you. He's there like a spare part, waiting for me to break down."

"Brian, that's horrible! Patrick's a human being! He's got nothing to do with you!"

"No, it's . . . you can't see it, but . . . That's where it's going. I'm gonna flunk out. It's coming. There he is, gifted as shit. He'll get into Harvard or something. I'll look like dog crap next to him. Dad . . ." he suddenly began some kind of great struggle, arms and legs straining. Sarah looked over and realized he was just shifting position to talk to her better. "See, I always knew!" He cried. He looked very flushed, or else it was the sunset. "It's like *Rosemary's Baby*. I knew from the time he was born. He had all of you fooled. I know why you and Mom are so crazy about him. 'Cause he looks so sweet and fucked up. Like he can't tie his own shoes. But thass a trick!" He was literally spitting on himself in his excitement. "I could see it in his eyes when he was two years old. Like how an alligator looks at you when he's half underwater! I'm gonna get you. . . . I'm gonna get you. . . ." He turned around to face the hedge again and upended the bottle for several seconds. "Do you want to know the real reason I had to fly down here?" He wiped his mouth with his arm.

"Oh, no," Sarah said. "You didn't wreck your new car?"

He laughed. "I tried to drive it up a tree. It didn't work."

"How much have you been drinking while you've been away?" Sarah asked. "Because that would explain your grades and the car and—"

"Sarah," he interrupted. "Shut up. If you were me, you'd drink too. Believe me."

The sky was now a deep purple. All that was left of the sun now was a thin strip of red on the horizon. The half-moon appeared, faint and miserable-looking. She didn't really understand exactly what Brian was trying to say, but she could feel his feelings. It was a cold wall of hate for Patrick, without a trace of remorse or regret. It had been there for a long, long time, getting worse and worse. She had never, until now, understood how serious it was.

"I tried to kill him three times," Brian said to the hibiscus.

Sarah looked over, afraid to speak.

"Nobody knew about the first time. He was two. Maybe even he doesn't remember it. I put a pillow over his face. I'd seen it on TV. Only on TV it happened fast. But he kept struggling around so long, I couldn't take it. I let him up. He was coughing and choking. I made him swear not to tell anybody. But he probably didn't remember anyway. While he was coughing and gulping water—I brought him water—I just kept thinking how stupid I was. Maybe I had been real close. Maybe if I'd just waited another minute, I could have gotten him."

"Oh, Brian, you don't mean any of this! You were four years old. You were just playing rough and—"

"Sure, sure. The second time you might remember. Wait." He tipped up the bottle and finished it. "We went on vacation to Disney World? You were about two then. He was six. Maybe you wouldn't remember. By the pool?"

Sarah shook her head. Her only memory of the trip was a horrible fear of the big costumed animals.

"Hotel pool. We were horsing around in the water. Holding each other under. I thought, *Hey, hold him down too long. Accident.* So I started doing it. He was strong. He was kicking and . . . but the good thing is, he was trying to scream, and that made him suck in water. You don't remember this?"

"No," Sarah said softly.

"But Mom was sitting in a deck chair with you. She caught on. She yelled at me to let him up, but I was like . . . carried away. I was on a high. I just sort of . . . laughed. And she could see it. She jumped in the pool and pried my hands off him. He was coughing like crazy, crying. He sort of vomited or something. I'm not sure. And Mom got him squared away and then she went ballistic on me. Well, not that I blame her. But it was a hotel pool. There was about a million people, a million *women* sitting around with their kids. But Mom hauled me out of the water and pulled my trunks down and spanked the daylights out of me. She could have taken me up to the room. And you know what I saw when I was pulling my trunks up? When I was dying of shame? Sweet little Patrick *smiling* at me. 'Cause he'd won."

"Brian! You—"

"Don't you see? He was fine. He swallowed a little water and then he was fine. She couldn't do enough for him the rest of the trip. *I'm* the one who got hurt. *I'm* the one who got humiliated."

"Brian, for God's sake! She was furious with you. You were . . . trying to hurt your own brother. Didn't you feel—"

"Ask him what he feels for me. Did he jump at this chance to steal my girlfriend? He'd do anything to hurt me, destroy me. But he doesn't get caught at it like I do. He's *better* at it than me. Don't you see?"

"Brian, you should get help. These kinds of feelings—"

"I didn't tell you about the third time yet. Don't you want to hear about all three times?"

It was dark now. All the shadows had faded from the grass. Some kind of little insect revved up and began humming rhythmically. "I don't know if I do or not."

He sat up and turned to her. "You gotta hear the whole story. It's so interesting! The third time was last year."

"I don't want to hear it!" Sarah put her hands over her ears. "I don't want to know this stuff!"

"Yes, you do!" He said viciously. "You're always dying to know everybody else's business. This should be a picnic for you." He reached over suddenly and grabbed her wrist, wrenching it down to expose her ear. "Now, listen to me! Okay?"

Whatever he tells me, I'm going to tell Mom, Sarah thought. *And she can decide what to do with him.* "Okay," she said softly.

He smiled. "Last year, when I was teaching him to drive. We drove way out of town, out past Flamingo

Road. Really into the Everglades. And the first thought I had was, '*I could leave a body out here and it would be a long time until they find it.*' "

"Why are you telling me this!"

"Shut up! Listen to me. I told him we ought to just park for a while by this canal and enjoy nature. Of course he went for that. Any wimpy activity turns him on. So we sat in the grass and he was just happily scanning around for egrets and I was scanning around for a big rock—"

"Brian, you're making this up."

"Am I? Anyway he lucked out because there was nothing around I could use."

Sarah had the feeling suddenly that all this was false, a bid for attention. "Didn't you think to get something out of the car?"

"Huh?"

"There's a tire iron in the trunk. Why didn't you go get that?"

"Well, obviously if I was messing around in the trunk, he'd want to know why."

"So what? Even if he caught on, even if he'd tried to run, you can outrun him. He probably didn't have much of a place to run anyway, and he would have been scared to try driving away and leaving you. You had him. You could have run him down, belted him and dumped him in the canal or swamp or whatever. You dope."

He closed his eyes briefly. His voice became dull and flat. "You don't believe any of this."

"You're telling me your fantasies, Bri. That's all. And they're scary enough. But don't act like they're real."

"Ask him! Ask him about the other times! Ask him if he thinks I could kill him. Do I have to kill him to prove it?"

Now, more than anything, Sarah wanted to "read" him. But it was just like Cissy said: Now that her emotions were involved, she didn't have a clue. She reached over, touched his arm. "Brian . . . I think you should talk about these feelings with Mom or Dad. And maybe think about—"

"Fuck you!" he exploded. The wine bottle flew wild and shattered against the fence. Sarah's body went rigid. Before she could react, Brian slumped down and began to cry into his hands.

Scared, Sarah just watched.

His shoulders heaved several times, and then he became motionless, still covering his face. Sarah touched his arm again. He didn't react. Finally he took a shuddering breath and looked up. "I'm an asshole when I drink."

"Got that right." Sarah tried to sound calm. Her brother was a total stranger to her.

"Have you got a Kleenex?" he murmured.

She shook her head.

He sniffed loudly. "Anyway you're right. All that was total bullshit. I never did any of those things. I just . . . I don't know. For a minute it made me feel like a big dick, talking that way. I don't know. I'm drunk. I'm stupid. I'm a failure."

Sarah felt very confused. "You're not."

"Not yet. But I will be. Don't you worry. I will be." He looked at her earnestly. With his lashes wet he resembled Patrick even more. "I'm sorry I scared you,

Pixie. That was a totally shitty thing to do. You shouldn't have stayed around to listen."

"Hey." She laughed nervously. "If it helped—"

"It didn't, but"—he got up suddenly—"you tried anyway. You're the only one in this family . . . at least you try. Don't tell anybody I was drinking and raving like that, okay?"

She looked up at him. In the moonlight his face was all strange planes and angles. Like something cut out of paper. She didn't know him. She didn't know a thing about him. She didn't know which of the many faces he'd shown tonight was true.

"I'll clean up the glass tomorrow," he continued.

"I'll clean it up now," Sarah said. "You've had a bad day."

"Bad life," he said faintly. He walked slowly back toward the house, like an old man. "Don't cut yourself," he muttered.

Sarah took a trash bag out to the hedge and carefully picked up the shards of green glass. They were easy to find in the moonlight. When she went in the house, Brian was nowhere around. Her mother had just gotten home from work and was looking in the refrigerator. "Are you hungry?" she asked.

"Look what time it is!" Sarah said. "Where have you been?"

"I told you this morning. We had a late staff meeting."

"Where's Daddy?"

"I don't know, dear, but he's a doctor. You know as well as I do we have to expect him when we see him. What's wrong with you? You look angry."

"It's after dark! You guys are never home!"

"Sarah! What's the matter with you?"

"I . . . Mom? Did you ever spank any of us when we were kids?"

"What?"

"I thought you and Daddy didn't believe in it. I thought we were never spanked."

"I'm having trouble following you."

"It's important. Did you ever . . . you know, lose your temper and do it anyway?"

"Once or twice with Brian, I think. He was more rebellious than you and Patrick."

"Can you remember anything in particular?"

Mrs. Shaheen took out a head of lettuce and gazed at it. "When we went to Disney World. Do you remember that vacation?"

"Barely."

"I spanked him by the pool. I remember that. I was furious."

"Why?"

"He had a little toy raft and he wouldn't share with Patrick. He made Patrick cry. And when I told him to share, he said '*No!*' just like that. To tell you the truth, I was embarrassed in front of the other mothers, having my child talk back to me like that. As I recall, I really lit into him."

"He wouldn't share a toy? That was it?"

"Yes, I think so. What is this about?"

"Never mind."

"Would you eat a tuna salad if I made it?"

"No, I had a horrible day. I'm just going to my room to read."

"Suit yourself."

Sarah took a long, hot shower and put on her favorite nightgown. The one with the rosebuds and the pink ribbon trim. Then she stretched out on the bed with her blank book. *It's impossible to ever find out the truth about anything*, she wrote.

Eleven

The last two days of Shadow's life had been spent on the sun porch. Sarah took literally Dr. Metzger's recommendation to give Shadow a weekend "filled with love."

The sun porch was Shadow's favorite part of the house. It was where she took her "deep naps" in the late afternoon, carefully calculating a patch of sunlight that would stay put for a few hours. Then she would paw and prod her favorite blue towel into a little round nest, curl into a tight ball with her tail covering her nose, and sleep the afternoon away. On weekends Sarah would join her, bringing a novel or a blank book and reading or working until she felt drowsy too. Sarah could see why Shadow loved sleeping there. The breezes and smells of outdoors gave a rich texture to Sarah's dreams. Often she had the recurring dream of flying over the Everglades, looking down on marshes full of exotic flowers and delicately tinted water birds.

Most of the family, except Patrick, thought Sarah

was torturing herself, making such a production out of the end of Shadow's life. They would break into the camp and offer outings and alternatives. "The cat's asleep, dear, and you look exhausted," her mother had said. "Why don't you come and get some ice cream with me?"

"Next week," Sarah said. "When Shadow's gone, I can go get ice cream all I want." Although she knew that next week she wouldn't want ice cream. In fact she knew that it would be a long time before she ate ice cream, just because they had discussed it here and now, under these circumstances.

"What is that crazy tape you're playing?" Dr. Shaheen had asked.

"The Talking Heads," Sarah said. "It's Shadow's favorite."

It really was too. Whenever Sarah played the tape, Shadow would listen, turning her ears this way and that like satellite dishes, picking up the rise and fall of David Byrne's voice. Shadow's favorite song was "Wild Life." She always closed her eyes and purred when the line came on about sleeping on the interstate.

Everything else on the sun porch was designed to cater to Shadow's whims. The bowl of kitten food she preferred to her adult catfood, which was normally reserved for special occasions. All her best mice and rats, from satin to denim. Her long-toothed flea comb. Her towel, freshly laundered and lightly sprinkled with Sarah's Tribe cologne, because Shadow liked the smell of Sarah. Even the wastebasket from Sarah's room was transported to the porch. Once in a while Shadow liked to climb inside and pretend she could tunnel through the bottom.

Of course Shadow was weak and hardly in a mood to enjoy her favorite things, but Sarah knew she appreciated the gesture. Shadow hardly ate at all now, but she had politely investigated the kitten chow and sniffed it deeply, remembering past treat times. Once, she had gingerly sucked a few pieces, all the while looking lovingly at Sarah. She ignored the toys but loved the towel, wrapping herself up in it like a cocoon. Periodically she would hop up into Sarah's lap and Sarah would comb her gently, trying not to notice the thin body under the thick fur. Sometimes Shadow would look into Sarah's eyes and purr with understanding. Sarah cried from time to time, but Shadow seemed resigned and even contented with her fate. Most of the time she appeared to be reassuring Sarah instead of the other way around. Sarah thought it was very possible that animals knew more about death than people did, considering how gracefully they prepared for it.

Most of the time Shadow looked out at the backyard. She gazed at the treetops, where the bluejays scolded her mercilessly as if they thought she were still a threat. She looked intently at lizards and spiders and squinted up into sunbeams. Sometimes she would close her eyes and sniff deeply, as if the smells of the yard needed to be memorized.

Lots of times she would just gaze at Sarah.

Patrick was the only one who would come and visit the sun porch. The rest of the family only stopped by briefly to bring Sarah food and check on her sanity. But

Patrick paid one long visit on Saturday and one on Sunday. On Saturday, when Sarah had been doing a lot of crying, he tried to be funny. On Sunday, when she was more composed, he spoke to her seriously. "This is a very special thing you're doing for her, and she knows it. You can tell."

Monday morning he was the one who drove her over to the vet. He was the one who helped her plan the funeral and he was the only guest. He was the one who insisted Sarah be allowed to take a week off from school.

He was also the only one who ever cried over Shadow besides Sarah. It was months after Shadow had died. Mrs. Shaheen was at the front door accepting a pizza delivery. Patrick, coming through the room with his nose in a book, had stopped suddenly and said, "Hey, don't leave the door standing open like that . . ." and then he realized his mistake. He looked anxiously at Sarah, then turned and ran back to his room.

Sarah had written all this in her blank book last winter. She had scribbled the details frantically, sometimes illegibly, along with fragments of unfinished, raging poetry. She read it all over now, sitting on her bed in the silent house, letting tears flow freely as she allowed herself, for the first time, to remember what the raw pain had actually felt like. She bowed her head and wept until her pajama top was splattered with tears. This time crying did some good, actually released the pain inside her instead of just making her head ache and her thoughts go numb.

When she finally ran down, she set the book aside and lifted her head slowly.

There was Shadow, sitting on the cedar chest at the

foot of Sarah's bed, watching her calmly. Not like a ghost, not like a hologram, like a big, furry, healthy black cat, watching her with a cocked head and a concerned expression.

Sarah held perfectly still, as if moving would dispel the image. "I'm not crazy, am I?" she whispered to the cat. "You really are here. You're back for some reason, aren't you?"

The cat didn't move or do anything, but in the eyes there was a wise humor.

"What is it, Shadow?" Sarah whispered, barely audible. "Why did you come back now? Is it like Cissy keeps saying? Did you come back to do something? Some specific thing?"

Almost mockingly the cat cocked her head the other way.

"Shadow, you'll always be my best cat. I might have other cats, but not like you."

Shadow closed her eyes in easy contentment. She took this for granted.

"I'm having a hard time getting over you."

The telephone rang beside Sarah's bed, an ugly, jarring jangle of sound.

"Damn!" Sarah shouted, and somehow she must have looked away because Shadow was not there. Just a cedar chest with a quilt on top. No depression in the quilt. Summer breezes stirred the curtains.

"Damn," Sarah said again softly. She picked up the phone. "Yes?"

"That's a nice welcome home! Maybe I'll just go back to Orlando!"

"Julian! Oh, God!"

"Wow. You really missed me, huh?"

"Julian, can we get together? Right now? Today? It's very important!"

"Sure. Whatever you say."

"I'll get dressed and bring my bike over. Okay?"

"You got it."

"Thank God you're home! I've been going crazy!"

"Boy!" he said. "I'm gonna go away more often!"

Julian's bike tire went flat halfway to the park, so they walked their bikes along in the hot sun. Julian didn't even seem to perspire, but Sarah felt like a wrung-out washcloth.

"I've got some crazy stuff to tell you," she began as they trudged along. He had finally gotten tired of describing all the artificial thrills he'd bought for himself at Disney World and Epcot and the Universal Studio theme park.

"More of that cat business?" he asked, squinting down at his tire.

Sarah was irritated at his tone. "Yeah. More of that 'cat business.' What? You don't want to hear it?"

He shrugged.

"You think I'm going nuts," Sarah said. Wet strands of hair tickled her forehead. She clawed at them.

"I just wish you'd go on to something else," he said. He was walking ahead of her, so she couldn't see his face.

"This isn't exactly something I'm doing by choice," she said. "This is something that's happening to me. Do you have to walk so goddamn fast?"

He stopped and turned, startled. "You don't have to talk to me like that!"

"I don't have to talk to you at all," she said, hurrying up so that she could go past him. He could just look at her back for a while.

He made some kind of noise behind her, a sigh. As if it really exhausted him to put up with her.

I hate him, Sarah thought. Even though the weight of the bike was killing her and she could feel the sun melting her sunscreen and cooking her face, Sarah trotted to the park entrance. She was seized with a desire to be childish. She almost wanted to see how Julian would react to childish behavior.

"One admission," Sarah said loudly to the park attendant.

Julian wheeled up behind her, puffing. "I'll pay hers," he said.

"You will not!" Sarah dug into the pocket of her jeans—a very tight squeeze—and pulled out a crumpled dollar bill. Then she got up on her bike and pedaled into the park, knowing he couldn't possibly keep up with her. She stood up and pumped hard along the bike path, to the first bend in the river. Then she parked and sat down in some shade waiting to see what he'd do.

After what seemed like a long time he appeared, marching along, still dragging his deadweight bike. He was definitely sweating now. He gave Sarah a frown when he saw her, but came to her, chucked his bike roughly into the grass, and let himself drop down next to her.

Sarah gazed at the sun reflections on the river. It looked like layers and layers of silk scarves, flowing in different directions. On top of that there were tiny points of brilliance, dancing and dancing. She pretended Julian wasn't there.

He untied the bandanna from his wrist and mopped his face. Then he smacked the piece of cloth against his palm several times. "You're mad at me, huh?" he said after a while.

She shrugged.

"What'd I do?"

She turned and looked him in the eyes. "You're supposed to be my friend, and I have stuff I need to talk about, and you act like, well, that's not an interesting topic so you don't have to listen. When you need to talk about something, like your relationship with your father—"

"Okay! Okay!" He winced. "Let's don't bring that up." Once, in a moment of weakness, Julian had confessed embarrassing and terrible details about his fights with his father. Sarah was careful never to let him forget it. "You want to talk about the cat, let's talk about the cat. What's she doing now? Throwing dishes around in your kitchen?"

Sarah gave him a look and then focused her eyes on the patch of dirt between her feet, preparing to confess. "I haven't told you everything, Julian. I mean, you were gone for a while, but all summer, stuff has been going on. That day we were at Loxahatchee and I got lost in the trails, Shadow appeared to me and showed me the way out." She looked up to see his reaction.

He was just staring at her. His brown eyes were calm and inscrutable. It could mean he was taking her seriously. Or it could mean he just knew he was hearing serious craziness and had better not joke around. "You saw a cat in the woods," he clarified.

"I saw Shadow. I know my own cat."

"And the cat showed you how to get back to the main trail."

"Walked ahead of me. Well, I saw it was Shadow, and of course I ran after her. So she led me."

"You were pretty upset at being lost. Maybe—"

"Maybe. But I know what I saw."

"Okay. Anything else?"

"Lots of else. I've been having dreams about Shadow. Hallways and doors and glass breaking. Shovels and coffins and blood and sometimes . . . naked people."

"Oh, jeez!" He looked away.

"Not like . . . look at me!" She smacked his arm. "Not like *those* kinds of dreams. Like . . . I can't explain it. This is some kind of message. Shadow is always in the dream, leading me down a hall, showing me . . . bad things behind doors and images of . . . like death things . . . graves, crosses . . ."

"This is just a lot of bad stuff you have on your mind. You've been thinking about the cat and her death. Graves. Hallways and doors. That's what everybody sees in dreams. Sex . . . well, you've got a hormone imbalance. Crosses . . . you were raised Catholic and you'll be haunted by that stuff forever. Why don't you have dreams like me? Last night I dreamed I ordered blueberry pie in a restaurant and they gave me lemon, but instead of sending it back I was digging all around in the lemon stuff looking for blueberries. That's a normal dream. You know what it is, Sarah? Stephen King. You

142   *Shadow*

gotta quit reading that stuff. Didn't you just read *Pet Sematary* this spring?"

Sarah had folded her arms and was calmly waiting for him to shut up. "Do you want to hear what else? Or does this stuff all scare you so badly, you have to try to explain it away?"

He looked down and smiled a small smile. "Go ahead."

"Cissy and I decided to hold a . . . sort of sé-ance. . . ."

"Oh, Jesus!"

"Not like in the movies. We just sat in a dark, quiet room and concentrated and she told me to . . ." Sarah still got the shivers remembering it, "call your cat."

His eyes lifted slowly. "Yeah . . ."

"I saw all kinds of things, Julian. I don't think I want to tell you everything I saw, but Cissy said she thought I had . . . a little bit of the same kind of ability she has. . . ."

"You think you saw visions?"

Sarah paused. She looked into Julian's eyes. "Yes."

Julian paused. "Really, Sarah?"

She felt sort of . . . free, telling the truth out loud. "Yes."

"You didn't see pictures in your head. You saw things in the room in front of you."

"Y . . . es."

"Did you hear things?"

· "Hear?"

"Did you hear voices or sounds in the room?"

"No. I heard *ideas* in my head."

"What did you see?"

"I saw . . . heaven."

"Christian heaven?"

"Cat heaven."

He bit his lip. "Oh, Sarah."

"How do you know?" she shouted. "How do you know I didn't? How do you know such a place doesn't exist?"

"Because it sounds like a little kid's fantasy!"

"Well, maybe little kids' fantasies are based on real things that adults can't see!"

"I don't know. I don't know anything. What else do you think you saw?"

"I saw Shadow and I talked with her."

"Talked?"

"She put ideas in my head."

"Okay. Like people say aliens talk to them during close encounters. Like telepathy."

"Yes."

"What'd she say?"

"She said . . . well, it's hard to explain what she said really. I mean, I think she sort of said she was staying with me because of something that's going to happen. And then she showed me the same kind of stuff that's in my dreams. It's . . . I feel like a bad thing is about to happen, and Shadow wants to protect me from it."

"I think Cissy's putting all this stuff in your head, and you're swallowing it up because you don't want your cat to be dead."

"Well, of course you'd say that." Sarah plucked a tuft of grass and threw it in the river.

"Sarah, you're telling me something crazy and asking

me to believe it. What kind of a friend would I be if I didn't tell you what I really think?"

Sarah sighed. "I don't know." Sarah spotted a bittern, posing as a reed on the opposite shore. The moment she realized what it was, it broke into motion, rising and flapping heavily off into the woods. How did it know she had seen it?

"Maybe I just want you to change the subject, Sarah," Julian said quietly. "You've been so obsessed with this stuff all summer, you don't notice anything else."

Something in his voice made her turn. Julian was gazing off across the water. The sun made his skin look golden. For the first time she saw a little fuzz on his upper lip. "What should I be noticing?" she asked.

He gave an exaggerated shrug. "I don't know! But we're going to high school next year! That's a big deal! We should . . . I don't know, talk about stuff." He looked at her.

"Stuff?"

"Well . . . we've been hanging out together all these years. But . . . you know, is that the same as *going* out?"

"Going out?"

"Going out! Going out! Going out!"

Sarah had never felt so wonderful in her life. She had been waiting for years for this moment. And Julian was just as delightfully embarrassed as she'd dreamed he'd be. "Well, I think it's like this," Sarah said. "If we *call* it going out, it's going out."

"Well . . . so, does that mean we're going together?" he insisted.

"If you want to. It's fine with me. But, I mean, we've never even kissed each other or anything. . . ."

"We can fix that!"

For the first time all summer Sarah was not thinking of Shadow. "Let's fix it right now," she said, leaning forward.

Julian leaned stiffly, closing his eyes. His lips brushed Sarah's mouth. Then he came back again, another pass, just grazing. Like someone tasting something. The third time his mouth was partly open. He pressed harder, putting his arms around Sarah. She brought her hands up and rested them awkwardly on his back. A wonderful, warm, comforting sensation filled her. She felt as if she were remembering something from a long time ago.

Julian pulled slowly back, opening his eyes. "You're good," he said in a low, soft voice.

"You're good too," Sarah said.

"I always thought you were special. I always knew it."

By way of answer Sarah cuddled into his arms. They stayed that way a long time.

Walking their bikes back home in the blaze of a Florida sunset, Sarah turned to Julian suddenly. "You must believe me deep down!" she said. "If you thought I was crazy, you wouldn't want to go with me!"

"No," he said. "I don't know if I think you're crazy or not. The thing is, Sarah, I like you so much, I don't care."

Sarah frowned slightly, then turned back toward the brilliant sky and trudged on.

Twelve

I'm in love, Sarah wrote in her blank book. Of all the things she'd ever written in the scores of blank books she'd owned since she was seven years old, this had to be the blandest and most unlyrical three words. But they were the most important, she knew. When she was a sixty-year-old woman, reviewing all her childish writings, this would be the page that would make her stop and smile. Sarah paused to picture herself at sixty. She hoped she would be an eccentric old lady, the kind who wore interesting hats and had traveled all over the world. Maybe she would be Julian's wife and they would have grandchildren together. Their kids would look Puerto Rican, she decided. They would inherit Julian's Latin looks and her curly hair. She pictured herself at some chic Miami restaurant, a slim, well-groomed woman with a little fake-leopard hat, having lunch with her grown daughter, Juanita. She would be lecturing Juanita, pointing her finger at her over the lobster salad, telling her she'd better get her life in order. She pictured Juanita rolling her eyes. *God,* Sarah thought. *I'll probably be just like Mom!* At first it was a chilling thought, but it also gave her a little swell of pride. Sarah made a note to write a short story about herself at age sixty having lunch with her daughter, Juanita. She added in the margin, *leopard hat. lobster salad. eye rolling.*

"Hey?" Patrick stood in the doorway to her room, balanced on one foot. This was his way of being polite. He had one foot raised to show that if he was intruding, he could immediately turn and sprint away, quick as a bunny. Patrick put most of his energy into being no problem to anyone.

Sarah finished her marginal notes before looking up. "Yes?" she said.

"Are you busy? Are you burning with the flames of genius?"

"Why? Do you need to ask me about the facts of life again?" Sarah grinned.

He stuck out his lower lip and spoke like a frightened child. "No. Your version scares me." He lowered his other foot to the floor, feeling welcome now. "Actually what I want is a woman's opinion on something. Okay?"

"Sure. Come on in." Sarah scooted over on the bed so that he could join her there. If Brian had come in, she would have stayed where she was, and he would have sat in her rocking chair.

Patrick sat at the foot of the bed, pulling his legs into a lotus position. He'd been very keen on yoga in his early teens, and this little remnant hung on. "I want to do something romantic with Karen. What do you think I should do?"

Sarah blinked. "Pardon?"

"See what a terrible world we live in? I say 'romantic' and you think about sex. And at your age too! I blame it all on the invention of the blow dryer. That's when our morals went down the drain. No, when I say 'romantic,' I mean *romantic* in the literal sense of the word. See"— he leaned forward a little—"she's been talking a lot about her and Brian and how . . . well, you know, stuff she didn't like about him."

"She really shouldn't say those things to you."

He straightened up. "Why not? He's ancient history. She's going with me now! But the main thing is, she keeps saying he was so unromantic. And as examples of this she's always pointing out how he took her bowling or out to play miniature golf. She says she never went anywhere with him where she had to wear a dress."

Sarah nodded. She could remember a lot of their "dates" that ended up in the Shaheens' living room watching TV. Sarah had made a mental note at the time never to date a boy who did that. There was plenty of time for that stuff when you were married.

"So, what she's telling me . . . I want to check this out with you . . . what she's telling me is that he was cheap, right? She'd like me to take her out someplace and spend some money on her. That's what she means by 'romantic'."

"Not exactly," Sarah said. "You don't have to spend a lot of money to impress a woman, but you have to . . . show a lot of thought."

"Huh?"

"Show you put a lot of thought into pleasing her. Lots of little things put together. Like, here's an example: A real fantasy date to me would be . . . okay, the guy would pick me up and give me flowers at the door. Flowers are great. If he got them at the florist, that's okay, but if they were wildflowers that he picked for me . . . see my point?"

"I do," he said. "Got a pen?"

Sarah laughed. "You'll get the idea. Okay, and then he would feed me in some fantastic way. Again, if he cooked for me, it would mean more than a four-star restaurant."

"I can't cook for her!" Patrick said. "Not in this zoo house with the fortune-tellers and trained bears walking in and out."

"You're right. Okay, I know. Get a little catered picnic and take it to the beach."

"Too hot for the beach."

"Not at night."

"Mosquitoes."

"Use a spray, for God's sake. Anyway, she'll put up with a few mosquito bites if the atmosphere is good. Or just park by the ocean and eat in the car. There, that's perfect."

"And it's a lot more private than a restaurant," he said thoughtfully.

"And after dinner, something like . . . something with the stars."

"You're sticking me out with the mosquitoes again!"

"No, wait! This is brilliant. Take her to the planetarium."

"Are you crazy?"

"No, I am not. Think about it, Trick. You sit in the dark with her and look up at stars."

"While some nerd gives a lecture on the Van Allen belt. No way. She thinks I'm a weird intellectual as it is."

"And obviously she likes that."

"Yeah, well, but the problem is, Pixie, *she* is not."

"I thought you were such an expert on Marilyn Monroe?"

"Huh?"

"All she ever wanted was for people to treat her like an intellectual, right? That's why she took the Method acting classes. And you even told me that's why she married Arthur Miller. If you take a bimbo like Karen—"

"Hey!"

"Well, a nonintellectual-girl-who-never-buttons-up-her-blouse like Karen to a planetarium, see what you're doing? You're telling her you think she's bright enough to understand it."

"I don't know."

"Imagine the darkness, the stars, that soft music they play."

"It's so weird, Pix."

"So don't be weird. Play miniature golf. If you don't want creative ideas, don't come in here."

He rocked himself gently, thinking. "Wildflowers, picnic in the car, and the planetarium. Would you like it if you had a date like that?"

Sarah allowed herself the luscious fantasy of doing those things with Julian. "I'd be putty in the hands of the man who took me on that date."

"That settles it. You're the closest thing to a woman I've got."

Sarah giggled. "Why don't you ask Mom's opinion? Or Cissy's?"

"Because Mom's idea of a fun evening would probably be to dress up like a Viking and pillage a town. And Cissy probably goes to her dates on a broomstick."

"That's not very nice!"

"She scares me."

"She does?"

He looked away. "Sort of." A blush spread over his face.

Sarah studied him carefully. "Do you like her?"

He unfolded his legs and stood up, massaging them to get the circulation back. "What kind of a stupid question is that?" he said. "I just said she scares me."

Sarah looked at him evenly. "I thought maybe that was why," she said.

Saturday night the whole family was in chaos. Dr. and Mrs. Shaheen were dressing for some kind of fund-raising gala, Patrick was readying himself for his planetarium date, and Cissy was trying to keep Brian from drinking her cooking vermouth. In the midst of it the Weather Channel was blaring into the empty living room because tornadoes had touched down in Palm Beach, and the whole storm looked as if it were heading directly for Coral Springs.

Sarah had taken up residence at the dining room table, where she could storm-watch out the big west window. There were two sets of fast-moving clouds at work, a pale-gray strip on the horizon that was pushing north to south like a freight train. Above that a mass of angry blackness with little hooks and whorls was sliding south to north. They circled each other in a slow, menacing dance. The cypress trees leaned down in the wind, and the bird feeder swung crazily.

A tornado warning is in effect for Palm Beach, Broward, Dade, and Monroe Counties. This means tornadoes have been seen in these areas. If you see a tornado, please go to a place of safety immediately.

"Here," Cissy said to Brian, taking the vermouth out of his hands. "Let me give you a beer or something, for goodness' sake."

"It doesn't matter." Brian listlessly relinquished her cooking vermouth and slumped even lower on his kitchen stool. "Hurry up, storm!" he called out drunkenly. "Come and blow this whole stupid family away!"

Cissy pushed a beer into his hands. "Hush! You want your mama and daddy to hear that?"

Brian hoisted the can, spilling some beer down his face. "Who the hell cares?"

Sarah looked away in disgust. He sounded like he'd been sneaking drinks all day. She wished her father would come out and see this. Always talking about how weak *Patrick* was.

Cissy was speaking to Brian in a low, confidential voice. "Did you ever stop to think you're giving him what he wants? When you look all upset and sit around drinking? That's just what Patrick wants. Why don't you show it doesn't bother you? Go call up some other girl.

Be proud. You don't want to sit around here looking like this."

There was a pause, and then Brian said thickly, "Would you go out with me?"

There was another, longer pause. "No," she said in a defeated voice. Then she walked off toward the laundry room, her heels tapping on the Mexican tiles.

Sarah resolved not to feel sorry for Brian no matter what. She decided to go and check on Patrick.

She knocked on their bedroom door. "Who is it?" Patrick called suspiciously.

"Me, you idiot."

The lock made a heavy, thunking sound. Patrick looked very South Beach; black jeans, white shirt, black loafers. Sunglasses would have been excellent, but considering the tornado weather, it might have been a little strange. As he walked away from the doorway and back to the mirror, Sarah noticed he seemed as much like a grown man as Brian. It was kind of spooky.

Patrick combed his hair several times, doing the same thing over and over. It looked perfect, but apparently not to him. "Well, I think parking on the beach is out of the question," he commented.

"Yeah, you'll have to . . . what are you going to do?"

"Junk the picnic. I'm buying her Italian. But the planetarium insists they'll be open. Of course, in a pinch she and I can find a storm shelter somewhere. If that isn't romantic, I don't know what is."

Sarah, curled up on Patrick's bed, picked at her sock. "Brian's getting drunk in the kitchen."

"How special. I'll be so sorry to miss it."

"Well, I'll get to see it all, I guess." Sarah sighed.

"Are you going to be alone with him tonight?"

"I guess so. When Cissy leaves."

Patrick turned from the mirror. "Stay out of his way, okay? He's really angry and he's been sitting in here drinking beer all day."

It hadn't occurred to Sarah to be frightened of Brian, but as soon as Patrick said it, it seemed like a possibility. "I just won't say anything to him."

"I'll tell you." Patrick started his hair all over again. "My worst nightmare is that he's actually going to flunk next year. If he gives up on college, he'll be hanging around here all the time, acting like a character in some Irish play. Ugh."

"Ugh," Sarah agreed.

"Okay." He turned from the mirror. "Am I beautiful?"

Sarah smiled. "You're always beautiful."

His smile went lopsided, his personal smile for her. "And they wonder why you're the pet of the family. Okay, I'm off."

"Patrick, are you getting ready to go?" Mrs. Shaheen's voice called from her distant bedroom.

"How does she know?" Patrick wondered aloud. "Yes!" he called back.

"Wait a minute."

He stood in the hall fidgeting. "Shit," he muttered.

Mrs. Shaheen came down the stairs in a purple-and-red spangled dress. There was something distressingly wrong with her hair. It was defying gravity. "Oh, sweetheart, you look wonderful!" she said to Patrick. "Look what that witch at the salon did to me. I look like the bride of Frankenstein, don't I?"

"Nobody will notice your hair if you wear that dress," Patrick said carefully.

"Sarah, what do you think? Daddy said it's okay, but I don't know."

"Daddy really loves you, Mom." Sarah giggled.

"Oh, great! Well, it can't be helped." She leaned over and kissed Patrick while he squirmed and resisted. "You have a fabulous time, sweetheart," she said, and retreated up the stairs.

"Jeez," said Patrick, wiping off her kiss. "Well, I'm going to go out and take my chances with the tornado. 'Bye, Pixie."

" 'Bye." Sarah tagged after him and watched out the front window. There was a drenching rain now. The wind whipped raindrops against the window. Patrick backed out of the garage into the downpour, windshield wipers on high. He waved at the house, then roared off with a dramatic splash of gutter water. The minute he was gone, Sarah felt worried.

Why were all these people going out in such a bad storm? It was like, once they had plans, nothing else mattered.

Sarah's father came down the stairs now, looking magnificent in his tux, tugging at his cuffs. Unlike most men, he loved to dress up. "Patrick leave on his date?" he asked, savoring the words. Ever since Patrick had started dating, his stock had been soaring.

"Yes, but the weather . . ." Sarah pointed to the TV

where a beautiful woman was pointing to a radar screen that flashed like Times Square.

Cissy came in, holding her car keys and a little pink umbrella. "I want to get going now, Dr. Shaheen, before this thing gets worse."

Sarah wondered if Cissy *knew* the storm was going to get worse.

"Sure thing," he said. "Where's Brian?"

Cissy shifted her eyes away. "He's taking a nap in the kitchen."

"A nap? In the kitchen?"

"Yeah. Well, you and Mrs. Shaheen have a good time at your party. I'll see you tomorrow." She opened the door, put up the umbrella, and dashed to the curb where her car was parked.

"Why wouldn't he take a nap in his room?" Dr. Shaheen asked Sarah.

"Patrick's been in there."

"Ah. Is Brian adjusting any better to . . . the thing about Karen?"

"I don't think so," Sarah said.

Dr. Shaheen folded his arms. "I never thought I'd see him be such a sore loser. It's disgraceful. Maybe I should go and have a talk—"

"Oh, Daddy, I don't think—" Sarah began.

Fortunately Mrs. Shaheen came down the stairs at that point. "Let's go, Bill, we're late."

He looked at his watch. "We are?"

"We will be, allowing for the rain-traffic. Sarah, be a good girl and keep all the doors locked. Is Brian staying home tonight?"

"He has to. No cars left."

"Okay, then I won't worry about you. We'll be home superlate, so don't wait up. And don't hang on the phone all night."

Sarah had never "hung on" a telephone in her life, but her mother seemed to have some persistent fantasies like that about her behavior. She was apparently remembering her own girlhood and assuming Sarah was the same.

"Drive carefully," Sarah said. They both hugged and kissed her at the same time, like a football huddle. Sarah went back to her window post and watched their big, ugly Lincoln maneuver out of the garage and slowly edge into the wall of rain. She picked up the remote control and flicked the TV off.

The house was very quiet.

Sarah hugged herself, listening to the rain pummel the roof. The living room was gloomy.

She went to the kitchen to investigate Brian. He was "sitting" at the breakfast-room table, head down on his arms, the way children take naps at their school desks. His beer can, empty apparently, lay on its side near his arm.

Sarah made a little noise of disgust. Brian had always been obnoxious, but this year he was outdoing himself. She placed her hand between his shoulder blades. "Hey."

"No!" he argued groggily.

"Why don't you go down to your room and sleep?" she said into his ear. "You'll mess up your back doing this."

"Can't," he said. His voice broke with self-pity.

"I'll help you," she said, tugging. "Come on."

He made a protesting wail, like a child being dragged into something dangerous. Then he looked blearily at his sister. "Sarah?" he asked.

"God!" she said. "You are far gone. How much have you had? Here, get on your feet." She looped his arm around her neck and hoisted him up.

"You're the only one who still cares, aren't you?" he asked, peering at the microwave as they passed it. He didn't seem to know what it was.

"Everyone cares about you, Brian. That's why we all want to kick your ass." She half walked, half dragged him down the hall to his room. He was very heavy.

The door was only partially open. Sarah kicked it wide. In doing so, she lost her grip on Brian, and he almost slid to the floor. Somehow, tilting him like a mattress, she managed to get him across the bed. He was facedown and angled wrong, but it was good enough for Sarah. "Can you get undressed by yourself?" she called. "I hope you can, because . . . good-bye!" She went out, closing the door after her. As she went down the hall, she heard him laughing faintly. He sounded almost insane.

Much as he disgusted her, Sarah felt lonely without him. She had never cared for being alone in the house. There was something else too. A bad feeling. A bad premonition. And what a night to have one, Sarah thought. Her parents and Patrick out driving in a dangerous storm, Brian drunk and angry. All sorts of things might happen tonight.

Maybe it wasn't a true premonition. It was just anxiety. Just normal psychology. Sarah hugged herself. It felt cold in the living room. She drifted from window to window, looking at the rain from different angles. The room was very dark now, but something kept her from turning on a light. She felt safer in the dark. She sat on the couch, facing the front door, and pulled her knees up to her chest. The rain was letting up. It made soft sounds on the roof now, like a tapping. Somehow that was worse than the heavy drumming. Even the storm was a kind of companion. If it ended, the room would be terribly quiet.

Sarah knew, suddenly, that Shadow was there. She just knew it.

The skin on her arms prickled. Stiffly she turned her head, scanning the deep shadows in the corners of the room, looking for an irregular shape or a sudden movement. The rain overhead was slacking, stopping. The wind whined suddenly, making Sarah jump.

"Shadow?" she called desperately. If something scary happened, it would be okay, but *waiting* for it to happen was almost unbearable. "Shadow, you're upsetting me! What do you want? Why are you here?"

The wind keened around the side of the house. Outside the front window trees were tossing and thrashing in the wind. They looked so helpless, rooted and unable to get away. Sarah's chest tightened. Something bad, terrible, was on its way, like a train coming toward her, and there was no one to help, no way to move. It was all going to happen, she didn't know what, but she could feel the situation, its cold, paralyzing terror. Shadow was here waiting for it, crouching somewhere in the dark, hiding.

Someone might die.

Sarah heard the words in her head, the complete sentence.

"Why?" she called out to her cat. Her voice was the impatient wail of a child. It occurred to her that this was all in her mind. She could be going crazy, having a breakdown. "Why won't you at least tell me, help me get ready?—" Sarah's voice broke, and she began to cry, her moans harmonizing with the shrill of the wind.

Thirteen

Sarah woke with a jolt, aware that she'd been vividly dreaming, but not sure what the dreams had been. For several minutes she felt disoriented, but gradually she realized it was still Saturday night. Patrick and her parents were still out, and Brian was sleeping it off in his room.

The VCR clock glowed in the dark living room. It was twelve-thirty. Sunday morning, then. A harsh, greenish light edged the furniture. Sarah felt chilled. She stood and drifted to the front window. There was a cold-looking full moon, high in the sky, casting a chartreuse wash across the front lawn. The air was clear. Sarah could see the rocks and bumps on the surface of the moon. She hugged herself. There was a taste in her mouth like metal. The harshness of the moonlight irritated her somehow, but she didn't want to turn on a lamp either. She wondered how on earth she could have fallen asleep. It didn't make sense. The last thing she remembered was that horrible storm and that she was anxious and crying, letting her imagination run wild. Would someone fall asleep right in the middle of that?

Sarah rubbed her arms, as if trying to restore circulation. She had the eeriest feeling someone had deliberately *put* her to sleep.

Before she could focus in on that idea, she was startled by a bright flash on the front window, turning the glass into a solid yellow glare. She heard a car pull into the driveway. Patrick's car. He got out, walked around, and opened the passenger door. Karen stepped out in a black dress so tight, she had to lean on Patrick to maneuver herself out of the car. As she regained her balance, she looked up at Patrick and giggled. He giggled with her.

Sarah felt annoyed. They were so mismatched and so stubborn about pretending they liked each other! What was he bringing her into the house for? Why hadn't he dropped her off? Sarah realized they must be planning to make out. It was logical. Patrick knew their parents would be gone for several more hours and he would expect Sarah to be in bed and Brian to be out cold.

Sarah backed away from the front door, feeling oddly guilty. She didn't want him to think she would wait up for him.

The logical thing to do was to walk off briskly to her room, but for some reason Sarah didn't do that. She backed around the couch and crouched down behind it. She wanted to hear what they would do.

Her face burned as she thought how shameful it would be if Patrick caught her, but something else in her was stronger. She had to do this. She locked her fingers together so that she wouldn't feel the tremors.

Hearing them open the door, she jumped from the adrenaline that shot through her. This was bad. A bad decision. There was a lifetime of perfect trust between Sarah and Patrick. He'd be furious. This was, almost, well . . . obscene.

Karen was giggling in a way that sounded very tipsy. "Are you sure this is a good idea, Tigger?" she asked Patrick.

Tigger! Even though no one could see her, Sarah put her finger in her mouth and pantomimed gagging.

Patrick's voice sounded congested and low. "It's a very good idea. It's an excellent idea. It's one of the best ideas I've ever had. Come here."

The couch creaked and gave as the two of them fell on it heavily. Sarah involuntarily drew back.

"Stop it!" Karen giggled insincerely. "Hey, I'm serious. What about Brian?"

"Forget him."

The couch shifted violently.

Sarah tried to imagine what position they were in and what they were doing. Patrick's inarticulate mumble sounded as if he had his mouth against Karen in some way. Every part of the couch was complaining. They had to be horizontal.

Sarah felt something like nausea in the pit of her stomach. She didn't want to be in on this. It was bad. It was dirty to listen to something like this. But . . . it wasn't exactly an unpleasant nausea. It was a very, very odd feeling.

Karen was making little noises of some kind, like kittens who can't locate their mother. "You like this?" Patrick asked in that same stupid voice Sarah hardly recognized. What was he doing?

"Mmm," Karen said.

"Tell me I'm better than him. Tell me you like me better than him."

Karen sounded like she was on drugs. "Him? Who?"

"Better than Brian," he insisted between kisses or bites or whatever he was doing.

"Better than Brian," she agreed.

Did fooling around make people retarded?

"No, no, hey," Karen protested weakly. There was the sound of a zipper. A long zipper. Her dress. Sarah felt heat in her face. She couldn't help thinking what it would be like to let a boy unzip your dress. It was . . . exciting. Like playing in some area the grown-ups told you was dangerous.

Rustling. Fabric rustling. "Tigger, no!" Karen laughed.

"Oh, you're beautiful. You are so beautiful. *Oh!*" She had apparently done something to him. What could a girl do to a guy that would get an exclamation like that? Sarah thought she knew. She had to shift around a little. She had an uncomfortable hot feeling all over. *I've got to get out of here*, she thought.

A short zipper. Only one kind of zipper that could have been. Sarah had never in her life felt so physically uncomfortable. And the sensation was definitely getting localized.

"We can't. . . ." Karen said.

"Yes, we can."

"Have you ever . . . ?"

"Don't worry about it."

"Yes, but you, I want you to be—"

"No problem. See?"

Sarah knew what that whole exchange was about. And she knew for a fact that her brother was about to have real-life, grown-up, man-and-woman sex not two feet from her. Her own body was throbbing, and she felt guilty and ashamed. This was the worst thing she had ever done. But if she moved now, he might see or hear her, and she didn't ever, ever want him to know she was doing this terrible thing to him. He was such a private person. He'd never be her friend again. He'd never trust her.

Karen made a moaning sound. Sarah's mind filled with pictures. Patrick and Karen, then Sarah and Julian. Julian's body with the moonlight skimming over those interesting contours men have . . . something hot and sudden happened deep inside Sarah, jolted through her repeatedly and made her feel she might be fainting. Then there was a bright light, filling the whole room. Her body was working out of control. Her mind dimly realized that someone had come into the living room and turned on the wall switch.

Brian.

Panting, trying to sit up (how had she gotten horizontal?) Sarah tried to focus her mind, but everything was slipping through it crazily, colors and shapes and ideas, punctuated with alternating jolts of terror and pleasure.

"You piece of shit." Brian's voice. Quiet. Deadly.

"Don't." Patrick's voice. Faint. Doomed.

"What the hell do you think you're doing?" Brian's voice was a little closer.

Sarah's head was clear now, her heart racing.

"I have a right to do anything I want with anyone I want!" Karen's voice now, loud and defiant. "Get out of here and give us some privacy."

"YOU PUT YOUR GODDAMN CLOTHES BACK ON!" Brian roared like a bear.

"Look," Patrick said in a very high-pitched voice. "You need to calm down. I know—"

"YOU DON'T KNOW SHIT! DO YOU KNOW YOU'RE A DEAD MAN? HUH? DO YOU KNOW THAT?"

Some kind of scuffle. Impact against the couch. Sarah pulled her knees up, making herself a tight little ball. She wondered if she could crawl unobserved to a phone and call 911. She wasn't sure what kind of emergency this was, but it definitely was an emergency.

"You leave him alone! Let go of him! You bastard!" Karen was quite a little fighter. Sarah was surprised.

There was a slap of some kind. Karen hitting Brian?

"YOU BITCH!" A terrible crash. Sarah couldn't hide anymore. She stood up. No one even looked at her.

Brian was holding Patrick by his shirtfront. Patrick had his jeans off, but thank God his underwear was still in place. He was shaking so hard, Sarah could see it from several feet away.

Brian looked crazed, dripping sweat, snorting like a horse, eyes glowing with rage. He had apparently just shoved or hit Karen to make her fall across the coffee table. She was sprawled there, with her backside up in the air, wearing nothing but a black lace bra and panties.

She began to cry. Mascara trickled down her cheek. Her black cocktail dress was crumpled on the floor. A rhinestone detail of some kind blazed in the lamplight.

Brian let go of Patrick, who was so shaky, he fell. "I'll get to you in a minute," Brian muttered. He headed for Karen, trampling her dress under his feet. Sarah remembered her dream.

Karen looked over her shoulder at Brian. "No," she moaned tearfully. But she made no move to escape. All the fight had gone out of her. Brian smiled and drew his foot back as if to kick.

Before Sarah could open her mouth to scream, Patrick came flying out of nowhere and landed on Brian's back like a monkey. "You leave her alone!" he growled.

Both boys went down on top of Karen and the coffee table. The glass top shattered. Sarah screamed.

This caused everyone to freeze. Karen came to life and worked her way out from under the body pile. Her arms and legs were cut and bleeding. Lace trailed like a lopsided banner down her leg. She grabbed her dress and ran for the front door, snatching Patrick's car keys as she went.

Sarah watched Karen's moonlit body sprint across the front lawn like something in a fairy tale. The car roared to life and careened out of the driveway.

Patrick was staring at Sarah, panting. "Where—"

He got no farther. Brian grabbed at him, trying to pin him down. Patrick's head hit the edge of the broken coffee table with a sickening *crack*. Patrick moaned.

"Stop it!" Sarah screamed. "You stop that, or I'll call the police!"

"You go to your room!" Brian said, trying to close

his hands over Patrick's throat. "This hasn't got any-thing to do with you!"

"You're rolling around in broken glass!" Sarah shouted. "You're both going to get cut to pieces!"

No one paid any attention to her. Brian was now literally choking Patrick, shoving his back into a pile of broken glass.

Patrick's eyes were wild and desperate. He brought his knees up and rabbit-kicked his brother dead in the groin.

Brian screamed, rolling over and curling up.

Patrick jumped up and tried to run, but he lost his purchase and fell in the glass again. There was a trickle of blood running down his neck. Sarah felt nauseated. The room was so hot, and she could smell blood. Her stomach pitched threateningly.

"You're dead now," Brian was chanting as he gath-ered himself up. "You are one dead little faggot." His hand clamped on Patrick's ankle.

Sarah looked around for something to hit Brian with. Maybe a vase? That knocked people out on TV, but would it work in real life? Maybe a heavy object would be better, but that could fracture his skull. Still, if he was about to kill someone . . .

Patrick was trying to slither away, making little kicks at Brian with his free foot. Brian grabbed that ankle as well, laughing softly. Patrick looked especially vulnera-ble in his underpants. It made him seem like a little boy.

"Sarah, for Christ's sake, call the cops!" he said.

Sarah started for the kitchen.

"Don't you dare!" Brian shouted, trying to look at

Patrick and Sarah at the same time. "Don't you dare do that to me!"

"Leave him alone, or I will!" Sarah called. "Let him go!"

To show she meant business, she stepped into the shadowy kitchen. She thought she saw something move near the sink, but there was no time to think about it because suddenly Brian's footsteps were pounding toward her. His hands grabbed her wrists, hot and rough. Panic surged. She twisted and tried to face him. He wasn't her brother at all. He was some kind of crazed male terror. She could hear his breath chugging like a locomotive. She could smell the sweat and alcohol seeping out of him. There was a jagged cut over his right eye that was nearly blinding him with blood.

"Leave me alone!" Sarah shrieked, looking around for a knife or anything to hurt him with. She would kill him if she had to. No one was going to hurt her. She was nobody's victim.

Patrick lurched up out of the shadows and kidney-punched Brian.

Brian groaned and let go, but Sarah stumbled and fell. Her ankle twisted under her in a red flash of pain. Meanwhile her brothers had toppled on the kitchen floor, punching and kicking like boys on a playground.

Sarah could see the wall phone. All she had to do was pull herself up. She held on to the edge of the kitchen table and tried to apply weight to her ankle. Her whole body shook. The pain was like fire. She slumped back down. Her brothers' brawl was escalating. She could hardly see, in the shadowy kitchen, who was who. They were tangled, rolling like a tumbleweed, both struggling for a pin. The grappling was punctuated every few seconds by a blow landing somewhere, a sickening, muffled sound like someone kneading bread or pounding meat.

"Stop it!" Sarah screamed, close to tears. "Stop it!" The wall phone was a long way away. She stared at it helplessly. She felt tears running down her face. Her ankle was swelling, the pain getting worse. She didn't feel she could move at all.

Something flickered at the edge of her vision. Sarah turned to look, but there was nothing. Suddenly the grappling sounds ended. There was nothing but the two boys panting.

Brian was on top, triumphant, holding Patrick down by his wrists, his knees clamped around Patrick's legs. Patrick had stopped trying to fight, was openly weeping. "Please . . ." he said.

Brian laughed.

"Leave him alone!" Sarah screamed.

Behind them, on the wall, something seemed to stir. A shadow rose out of nowhere, a black silhouette rearing up from nothing. The shadow of a cat.

It was just like in the movie theater, the sharp-angled, huge cat shadow projected on the wall behind the two boys. It seemed to pulse. The angles were as sharp as a paper cutout. Sarah whined involuntarily.

Neither of them saw it. Brian was staring down into Patrick's face with something almost like tenderness. The cut on his forehead dripped blood into Patrick's face.

Abruptly Brian let go of one wrist and drove his
fist into Patrick's jaw. Sarah winced. Patrick moaned
and went limp. Brian smiled. "That's a good boy," he
said.

He let go of Patrick's other wrist experimentally.
Patrick didn't move. He just sobbed quietly. Brian
laughed to himself. He placed his hands carefully, lovingly, on either side of Patrick's throat.

"No!" Sarah screamed to Brian. "Don't do it!" Then
she screamed at the shadow on the wall. "Don't let him
do it!"

The shadow on the wall had changed position. It was
crouching. A cat preparing to lunge.

Patrick's chest heaved. One of his hands clenched
and unclenched. His fingers raked the linoleum.

Brian shook him impatiently. "Hurry up and die!" he
growled.

There was a sudden gust of cold wind. The shadow
on the wall sprang.

Something cyclonic enveloped the boys, a whirl of
black fur and strange little glimmers of light. Brian
screamed and covered his face.

Patrick pushed Brian off and scrambled to his feet,
coughing and stumbling. He staggered out of the
kitchen. Sarah heard him run down the hall. He would
go to the bedroom, where he could lock himself in. A
door slammed. He was safe.

Some kind of strange quiet pervaded the kitchen.
There was no sign of the cat shadow anywhere.

Brian slowly took his hands away from his face. He
looked at Sarah with a stunned expression. In the dim

light she could see five tiny vertical scratches down the side of his cheek.

"Something jumped on me," he said softly. "An *animal* jumped on me."

Fourteen

Sarah felt old, heavy, and tired. Standing on one foot, she slumped over the bathroom sink, wringing out the washcloth over and over again, allowing herself a few seconds to savor the comforting drum of hot water on her hands. Down the hall, in the living room, she heard the clink of glass, another chunk of the coffee table hitting the garbage bag. What were they going to say to Mom and Dad when they got home? It could be any time now too. It was after two.

Crossing the hall, she tapped on Patrick's door. There was no answer. *Clink* from the living room.

"It's not him, it's me," Sarah said, rearranging the wet cloth in her hands so that it wouldn't drip.

"I'm all right. Leave me alone." He sounded hoarse.

"Come on. You're bleeding. Let me make sure you're okay."

"I'm okay."

Sarah shifted her weight. Her sore ankle throbbed. She was tired of older brothers acting like children. "You let me in, and I mean right now!" she said in a voice that could have been their mother's.

Something unpleasant-sounding was muttered on the other side of the door. The bolt unlatched noisily. Patrick was in a bathrobe—he never wore a bathrobe—holding a fistful of Kleenex against the side of his neck. Bright red blood was soaking through them. The front of his neck was marked with thumb-shaped bruises. "Where is he?" Patrick asked.

Clink. "He's cleaning up the glass. Then I guess we're going to shampoo the carpet, since it looks like something died out there."

He put out his free hand like a bar across the doorway. "Just leave me out of it. I'm okay. I want to be by myself for a while. All right?" He tried to close the door.

Sarah put her hand in the doorway. "Not okay," she said. "I mean, you don't have to help clean up or talk to Brian, but you have to let me work on that cut. Mom and Dad will be home any minute. You want me to examine you, or Dad?"

He sighed and stepped back from the door. Sarah came in and pushed him gently into a sitting position on the bed. She took away the Kleenex and washed his cut. It was small but deep. Sarah held the washcloth against the cut, waiting for the bleeding to slow down enough for her to put a Band-Aid on. "Brian has a gash over his eye and scratches down his face," she said carefully.

"I don't care."

"Did you scratch him?"

Patrick looked up at her and then away. There was a loud dragging sound from the living room, as if Brian was hauling the broken carcass of the table off somewhere.

Sarah checked her washcloth. Almost no blood flowing at all. She fished in her pocket for a Band-Aid. "Tell me what you saw," she said quietly.

"What do you—ow!—mean? I saw my brother try to kill me. What else would I see?"

Sarah tilted his head back to look at his throat. She had never seen anything so horrible. There would be no way to conceal this from Mom and Dad. If they even wanted to. "My God!" she said. She sat on the bed and applied the clean side of the washcloth to his throat.

"It's no big deal." He shrugged. "I always knew that was his goal. He's been talking about killing me for years. Nobody else ever took him seriously, but I did."

"He was real drunk. You should have seen him earlier."

"So? When you're drunk, you do stuff you would have done anyway. You just worry about it less. He's still a goddamn killer, and he ought to be locked up."

"He's acting weird now. Like he's in shock. I think he scared himself."

"Oh, yeah. Let's feel sorry for him."

"I do."

"Well, I don't. I think all the sympathy should be for the guy who couldn't breathe for a while."

"He didn't mean to hurt you that much. You know that."

Patrick's eyes were narrowed. "What's your theory? He just wanted to cut off my oxygen long enough to give me some brain damage? So we'd be equals again?"

"Sometimes people go a little crazy. Especially when they drink. He did stop." She glanced up at him.

He looked into her eyes. "He didn't stop on his own," he said flatly.

There was a huge, roaring silence between them for several seconds. "What made him stop?" Sarah said.

Patrick looked away. "We both know what made him stop. I saw her jump on his face. I saw her scratch him. And then she dropped down on me before she . . . went away. I felt her hit my chest. And . . ." He hesitated one more second and opened the top of his robe. Against his breast bone was a delicate, curved cat scratch.

Before Sarah could say anything, she heard a general commotion in the living room. Her parents' voices were exclaiming, and Brian was answering in a shaky voice.

"I don't want to talk to anybody until tomorrow!" Patrick said.

Sarah gave him the washcloth to hold on his bruises. "I'll do what I can."

Patrick slumped on his bed. He seemed to fall asleep immediately, as if drugged.

In the living room Brian was on his hands and knees, scrubbing bloodstains off the carpet with a sponge. Dr. and Mrs. Shaheen, looking strange and disoriented in their finery, were trying to understand what had happened without giving Brian any chance to talk.

"You need to take care of that cut on your face right now!" Dr. Shaheen said, throwing his dinner jacket on the couch and fussing with his cufflinks.

"How could you have an 'argument' that would shatter a coffee table?" Mrs. Shaheen demanded. "I want to know what really went on here and I want to know it now!"

Dr. Shaheen met Sarah in the doorway on his way to get medical supplies. "Are you all right?" he asked.

"I turned my ankle, but it's okay," Sarah said. "Patrick has some bruises and cuts. He was very upset. I think he needs to be alone for a while."

"Sarah, please come in here and tell me what happened!" Mrs. Shaheen cried.

"Let her go to bed. I'll tell you about it!" Brian said.

Mrs. Shaheen knelt down in her beaded dress and took the sponge away from him. "You're doing it wrong," she said. "You're working the blood into the fibers." She turned to Sarah. "Is Patrick all right?" she demanded. She didn't wait for an answer. "I don't understand why we can't go out one night of the year and leave boys who are supposed to be adults alone without finding the furniture smashed and blood everywhere." Abruptly she began to cry.

Sarah had never seen her mother cry before. Ever. It was too much. Sarah had had about as many different emotions as a person could stand in one night. She sat down on the rug where she was and put her face in her hands.

"Whoops!" said her father, nearly tripping over her as he brought a handful of medical supplies in. "Pull yourself together, Judy, we're all tired," he said to Mrs. Shaheen, who had already tamed her sobbing down to a sniffle.

"You don't know what we paid for this rug!" she joked weakly. She sniffed several times and went back to work on the stain.

Dr. Shaheen knelt and examined Brian's cut. Sarah felt herself relax. They were attending to things now. Everything would be all right. "Patrick's okay," she answered her mother's old question. "He was sleeping when I left him. We shouldn't disturb him."

"What could you have possibly done that broke the table?" Dr. Shaheen asked, dabbing antiseptic above his son's eye.

"I don't know," Brian said. He was taking on that dazed look again.

"Can I go to bed?" Sarah asked. No one answered her. She limped down the hall, glancing at Patrick's door as she went by. He could have died. A few more seconds and they would have had more to clean up than a coffee table.

In her room she stripped off all her clothes and fell across the bed. She wanted to write in her blank book, but there was too much, too many different things to say. She switched off the lamp and stared out the window. The moon had set. The night sky was obscured by a wall of angry, dark-green clouds. The darkness in Sarah's room was green.

Something felt different. Something had changed. The whole . . . focus of the world, the whole way the picture looked. She waited for a clear impression of what it might be, and then she knew. She absolutely knew.

Shadow was gone. She had come to rescue Patrick, to pay him back for the funeral. To pay him back for helping Sarah when she was grieving. She'd done what she came to do and now she was gone.

. . .

In the morning the sky was still overcast, and the light inside the house was still green and murky. Sarah woke up feeling bruised and tired. She stood up and tried her ankle. The soreness had lessened. Sarah put on a robe and drifted out to the kitchen table, where family members were slowly collecting like birds on a telephone wire. Cissy was standing at the stove, head down, scrambling eggs. Dr. Shaheen was pretending to read his paper, but his eyes never moved and he never turned a page. Mrs. Shaheen was glaring at Brian, who was supporting his head with both hands and breathing in the fumes of his coffee as if it were keeping him alive. The cut over his eye had swollen, making him look like some kind of tough character; a boxer or a longshoreman. The scratches down his cheek were like strings of delicate brown beads. Sarah took her seat and sipped at her orange juice, trying to read the mood and decide if she wanted to speak. She decided she did not.

Patrick came in last, standing in the kitchen doorway for a minute looking at his family as if they were strangers to him. There was something almost wild and feral about him, maybe because he hadn't bothered to comb his hair. He wore a white scoop-neck T-shirt, which framed the black thumbprints on his neck.

Dr. Shaheen looked up. "My God . . ." he said softly. He looked at Brian, who refused to look up.

Mrs. Shaheen and Cissy both looked at Patrick to see what was so shocking. Mrs. Shaheen gasped and started to get up.

"I'm fine!" Patrick said forcefully, holding up his hand. "Just leave me alone. What's the big surprise?

He's wanted me dead for years. He finally just got around to doing something about it."

Brian still didn't look up. "I don't want anybody dead," he said almost inaudibly.

Patrick circled his chair like a hawk before slumping into his own. "Well, you could have fooled me!" he growled.

"Did you do that to your brother?" Mrs. Shaheen asked Brian in a scary, quiet voice.

He rubbed his forehead. "I was drunk, okay? He was here on the couch *with my girlfriend*, and they were—" He broke off and shut his eyes tightly, then opened them and looked at Patrick. "I didn't mean to do it, Pat. I'm sorry. I'm so sorry. . . ." He choked up and looked at the table again.

Patrick lowered his head too. For once Sarah couldn't read his reaction at all.

Cissy took advantage of this silence to set plates in front of everyone. No one touched the food, and Brian shoved his eggs away, as if the smell bothered him.

"Let me go make the beds and give you all some privacy," Cissy said.

"No, wait," Sarah said. She looked at her brothers. "Tell them what else happened! Brian, tell them how you got the scratches on your face."

He kept his head down. "I don't know. Everything was flying everywhere."

"What did you say to me? You said an animal attacked you! Don't you remember? Look at his face!" she said to her parents. "Those are cat scratches."

"Oh, God," said Dr. Shaheen. He looked at Sarah as if she were crazy.

"Shadow was here!" Sarah said. "She jumped on them and broke up the fight! They both saw it as much as I did!"

Neither Patrick nor Brian would look up. Sarah wanted to kill them both.

"Sarah," said Mrs. Shaheen. "You've been through an ordeal. What happened last night must have been very upsetting."

"No!" Sarah turned to Patrick. "Tell them! Back me up! Show them the scratch on your chest!"

"I was confused," he said, still not meeting her eyes. "It was such a crazy. . . . We were all three rolling around clawing at each other. It was crazy. I just—" he looked up suddenly. "Can I be excused?"

His father touched his arm. "Sure."

Patrick fled, glancing fearfully at Sarah as he passed her.

"You coward!" she shouted after him.

"Sarah!" said her mother. "Don't you realize what he's been through?"

"Yes, I do!" Sarah said. "I was there." She looked at Brian. "What are you afraid of? After everything that happened, what difference does it make? Just say what you saw. I know you saw it."

"I was drunk," he muttered, not meeting her eyes. "The whole thing is a blur."

"Sarah, let's concentrate on what's important," said Mrs. Shaheen. "Like the fact that your brother is out of control and obviously needs help." She looked at her husband to see if he would confirm this. Dr. Shaheen looked ready to cry.

"I'll never take another drink as long as I live," Brian

said. "Don't you think I scared myself as much as I scared him? I know he gets to me, but I didn't know I would actually hurt him. I didn't mean to do anything like that. It's so horrible. I mean, I'll do anything to make it up to him. If I need to get in a program, or lock myself up or whatever. I'm not a bad person. I don't want to hurt anybody!"

"Of course you don't," his father said. "Look, sometimes a man gets out of control. If you saw him with Karen. . . . Men have feelings that are—"

"Oh, this is disgusting!" Mrs. Shaheen interrupted. "You will excuse absolutely anything in that boy. Men's feelings! Did you see the marks on Patrick's neck? You want to explain that away? It was . . . what? A crime of passion?"

"I'm not saying he doesn't need help!" Dr. Shaheen snapped. "He admits as much himself. But we know he's a good boy and we still love him, don't we?"

"I'll love him tomorrow," Mrs. Shaheen grumbled. "Today I'm not so crazy about him."

Brian hung his head. "You can't say anything to me I'm not saying to myself."

His father patted his hand. "It's going to be all right, son. Maybe it took something like this for both of you to see how destructive all this rivalry is."

"I don't hate him," Brian said to his placemat. "I really don't."

"We know," said Dr. Shaheen.

Brian was on the verge of tears. "I think I want to be excused too."

"Sure," said his father.

Everyone was silent until he was gone.

"He's not going to their room, is he?" Cissy asked.

"He slept in the guest room last night," Mrs. Shaheen said. "I would think he's going there." She turned to her husband. "Does Patrick need an examination?"

"I'll look at him in a minute. I think it's just terrible bruising and a bad scare. They may both need counseling before this is over. Maybe we all need family counseling. I don't know." He glanced at Sarah.

"You think I'm crazy, don't you!" Sarah said.

Mrs. Shaheen slapped the table. "Sarah, we can't deal with this now. There's too much else going on! Can't you see that?"

"Of course I can, but you can't treat me like I'm crazy. I'm telling you something miraculous that happened. Patrick might be dead if it weren't for Shadow." She looked at Cissy. "You believe me, don't you?"

Cissy pulled her shoulders back. "Yes, I do."

Mrs. Shaheen wheeled around. "Now, look! The last thing we need is to introduce a lot of voodoo into this horrible situation."

Cissy met her eyes fearlessly. "Just tell me it's none of my business and I'll leave the room. I know you're all upset about your boys, but you need to realize what else is going on. Sarah is special. You have to treat her specially. I know what it's like when everyone thinks you're crazy, just because you see things they don't."

Mrs. Shaheen raised her voice. "It's you who've been filling her head with this junk all summer! You knew she was upset about the damn cat and you've helped her feed this horrible fantasy! How am I supposed to teach her anything about facing reality when I'm undercut at every turn by some kind of irresistible Mary Poppins with a broomstick! Of course she wants to believe her cat is still here! I'd like to believe my father is still here! We all want to cling to these beliefs! But can't you see where it leads? Now she's seen something terribly traumatic and she's practically snapped!"

"I have not!" Sarah said. "I think I'm the calmest person in this house! Just because I'm saying something you can't agree with, that doesn't make me crazy!"

"I'm not saying 'crazy,' dear," Mrs. Shaheen said. "It's perfectly normal, when you see upsetting things, to retreat—"

"You're not a psychologist, you're a newspaper reporter!" Sarah shouted. "You don't know anything!"

Mrs. Shaheen sat up very straight. "Fine. Your father's a doctor. Let's hear what he thinks."

Dr. Shaheen was shaking his head. "I don't understand how things got this way," he said. "I thought we were a loving family. Why is everyone at each other's throats?"

"Daddy, you told me you saw a ghost once, didn't you?" Sarah said.

He blushed. "Well, I thought I did. But I could have been wrong. I was very upset. Just like you are now, Pixie."

"Why is everyone so afraid of this!" Sarah said.

"Because they don't understand it," Cissy said. "Because they can't see what you and I can see."

"That's enough of that and I mean it!" Mrs. Shaheen swiveled, and pointed her finger at Cissy.

Dr. Shaheen looked up at Sarah. "I really think if

you would just get yourself another cat, all this stuff would go away."

"Shadow already did go away. She came here to save Patrick's life, and as soon as she did, she was gone. I could feel it."

"You're right," Cissy said. "I don't feel her here anymore either."

"That's it!" Mrs. Shaheen said. "Get your things together and go!"

Cissy folded her arms. "Are you sure you mean that?"

"Yes, I do. I will not risk my daughter's mental health. Obviously you pander to—"

"I would like to stay here, Mrs. Shaheen. For two reasons. One, because I like this family very much. And two, because I understand some things about your daughter that you don't. She has a very special talent. And if nobody helps her handle it, it's going to be ten times harder for her."

"You go get a nine-hundred number and peddle that stuff to the weak people who need it," Mrs. Shaheen said. "I want you out of here. Now. Today. This morning."

"So, if I don't quit talking about this stuff, are you getting rid of me too?" Sarah asked.

"Give it up, Sarah," Cissy said, getting her purse. "You can't argue with a closed mind."

"I am very open-minded!" Mrs. Shaheen shouted. "I just know bull when I hear it."

"Please!" Dr. Shaheen moaned. "Can't we accomplish anything without shouting?"

Cissy halted in the doorway. "Just one more thing before I go. Because now I don't work for you and I can say what I want. The biggest problem you have, Mrs. Shaheen, is that Brian is a bully. Pure and simple. And that's why he makes you so angry. But you'd better ask yourself where he learned it." She turned to Sarah. "If you ever need to talk to me, look me up in the book. You're very talented, and there is not one single thing wrong with you. Except the family you were born into. Good-bye, Doctor." She closed the door gently.

They all listened to her car pull away.

"You are never to call her, do you understand?" Mrs. Shaheen said.

Sarah just looked at her. She felt more powerful than she had ever felt in her life. She realized that of all the people in this family, she, Sarah, was the strongest. It was just a matter of growing into it. She didn't even need to argue. Her parents couldn't control whom she called or whom she talked to. Or what she chose to believe. "Excuse me," she said.

As she left the kitchen, she heard her mother say to her father. "I am not a bully! The trouble is, I've given those children too much freedom!"

There was no answer.

Fifteen

Julian answered the door.

"I need a friend to talk to," Sarah said.

He nodded. "You want to go somewhere?"

"Yes. I want to go to a playground."

"A playground?"

"I want to pretend like I'm still a little kid."

They chose the playground at Tradewinds Park. Sarah liked swings with hard seats, not those rubber things that grab your hips. For the first twenty minutes she worked out her frustrations by swinging as furiously as she could. She could easily look over the top bar when she was at the apex. The wind rushing at her face gave her a feeling of freedom.

Julian respected her mood. He swung beside her in silence, waiting until she felt like talking.

Finally, when she had worked her muscles to the point of pain, she began to let the cat die. *Let the cat die*, she thought. She dragged her feet in the gravel. The soreness in her ankle was almost gone. "I'm going to climb on the jungle gym," she told Julian, and walked away.

Again he patiently followed, climbing up after her and sitting on the top with her. From this height they could see beyond the first bend in the river. The clouds had never lifted, so the air was unusually dusky and cool. A swarm of gnats hovered nearby. Sarah watched them, fascinated by their rhythm and the way they kept formation while constantly changing position. She wondered if they communicated.

Then she looked at Julian. He wasn't a member of her family. He was a clean, blank page where new things could happen. He squinted at some point in the distance, frowning slightly. His eyes were both fierce and gentle. She wondered if he had Indian blood. There was such . . . stillness in him. Sarah longed for stillness.

"I don't know where to begin," she said.

He swung his even gaze back to her face. "Anyplace is fine."

Sarah picked at her fingers. "A lot of crazy things happened last night. Patrick and Brian had a fight."

He laughed. "What else is new?"

"No. Not like the usual. Violent. Brian attacked Patrick. Patrick attacked Brian. There was . . . Karen was there. See, what happened, Patrick and Karen were making out on the couch—"

"In front of you and Brian?"

"No, they . . . came in and they thought they were alone, but I was . . . actually I was sort of behind the couch."

Julian blinked.

"I mean, when they came in and all, I didn't know what to do, so I panicked and got behind the couch."

He smiled. "So you were eavesdropping on them, and then what happened?"

She smacked at him. "I was not! You had to be there. Anyway they started . . . well, you know. And then Brian came in."

"Oh, boy."

"And after that it got crazy. All three of them were fighting and throwing each other around. . . . They all fell into the coffee table and smashed it."

"Oooh."

"Yeah, it was . . ." Sarah noticed her voice had gotten high. "There was blood and glass and . . . do you remember all the dreams I was having about blood and broken glass?"

"Yeah," he said. "That's really interesting."

Sarah felt encouraged. She hadn't known if she was going to tell him everything, but now she decided she would. "After the table broke, Karen took off in Patrick's car. And then the boys started . . . I don't know, Julian. They were all bloody, and it was like they were going to kill each other. So I decided to call the police, and then Brian went after me—"

"That son of a bitch!"

"He was really out of his mind. Worse than I've ever seen him. I think he'd been drinking all day. That's his excuse, anyway."

"Did he hurt you, Sarah?"

"No. I mean, I twisted my ankle, but it's okay. Patrick pulled Brian off me. . . . God, this sounds like some movie, not like people I know. . . . And then, okay, by that time we were in the kitchen, and Brian got Patrick down and punched him, and then"—her voice ran up the scale again—"he started to choke him."

Julian was breathing hard. His eyes were fixed on Sarah's. She knew she told stories well.

"And I saw Shadow. I saw her shadow on the wall, and she . . . jumped on them and made Brian let Patrick go. She saved his life. That's what she came for. She knew this fight was coming and she knew Patrick might get hurt and she came back to help him."

Julian was still breathing hard, still caught up. But something was happening to his eyes. Just a flicker of change. Of distaste. "Sarah," he said. Then he hesitated, as if he didn't know what to say. "Sarah, you've got to stop this."

Sarah felt cold. "Stop what?"

"Stop trying to do this. Trying to make things into something they aren't. I know you've had a rough time, and it sounds like things are worse at your house than you thought. But it doesn't help . . . I mean, it may make you feel better when you're scared to—"

"Did you even give ten seconds to trying to believe what I'm telling you?" Sarah said.

His dark eyes were solemn, flat. "No, Sarah, I didn't. I've been trying to go with this all summer, but deep down I know it's wrong. Dead animals are dead animals. They don't come back, and they sure don't come back and break up fights. Come on."

"Patrick and Brian saw her too. They won't admit it now, but last night they saw her. Patrick thinks she scratched him."

"So what? You're a very convincing person. Patrick's

a very sensitive guy. You've got him buying into your fantasy."

"No." She shook her head. "Julian, that's not what it is."

He reached over and touched her ankle. "Sarah, I really care about you. I love you. I wasn't planning to say that right this minute, but it's true. I think you're hurting yourself. Somebody has to talk to you straight."

Sarah felt dizzy. The park seemed to sway all around her. The clouds were like an oppressive wall, a prison ceiling, shutting out the sky. The movement of the gnats was maddening, insane.

She closed her eyes. She pictured carefully the kitchen last night. Then she opened her eyes again. "No," she said. "You're wrong. I know what I saw, and it doesn't matter if you think it's crazy. Cissy said—"

"Cissy!" he said with disgust.

"Cissy understands this. None of the rest of you do. She warned me how lonely I would feel. But I'd rather be different and misunderstood than give up something I *know* is true. I've been having visions and dreams and feelings all my life. I used to think they were my imagination, but I don't think so anymore. My cat was here with me this summer, and last night she did something miraculous, and now she's gone. I know that. If you can't believe it, that's your problem."

The wind was picking up. Julian glanced in the sky. Then he looked at his watch. "Nobody can ever help you if you don't want to be helped."

"I don't want to be helped. Your idea of helping is like amputation. You want to take something away from me that's perfectly good."

He held out his hands. "Okay. Fine. I think the subject is closed. You think what you want, and I'll think
what I want. It doesn't have to affect our friendship.
Does it?"

They looked at each other a long time. "How can
you say you love somebody when you don't understand
them?" Sarah said.

"I think I *do* understand you!" He said. He was leaning forward.

Sarah folded her arms. "You don't."

He looked up in the sky again. "It's going to rain."

"Do you want to go home?"

He looked down. His long lashes made Sarah want to
cry. "I guess so. Will you call me?"

"Maybe," she said. Immediately she felt a heaviness
in her chest. It was a feeling she remembered well. Grief.
Loss.

"Okay!" He said in the brisk voice of boys trying not
to cry. "Let's go!"

Sarah rode her bike behind his all the way back to
Coral Springs so that she could look at him and memorize every detail.

Back at home Sarah found Patrick's car in the driveway with a note on the windshield. She resisted the urge
to read it. Anyway she knew what it would say. A girl like
Karen wasn't going to mess around with crazy, violent
boys like her brothers.

At first she thought her house was deserted. But as
she passed her brothers' room, she heard male murmurs
behind the door. They were talking to each other. Qui-

etly. Rationally. Maybe Brian had come to apologize. Sarah found she couldn't care less. They were both traitors as far as she was concerned.

Behind her parents' door was another inaudible conference. *Probably my sanity hearing*, Sarah thought.

She stood in her dusky bedroom for a minute feeling very alone. She wished she could summon Shadow, but she knew it wouldn't work now. That was sadder than losing Julian.

She picked up her blank book, but for once in her life she was unable to write. She had too much to say. Or too little. Or she just didn't know how she felt at this point. She flipped back to the page where she'd written, *I'm in love*. She dated a fresh page and wrote, *I'm not in love anymore. Shadow's gone. Nobody understands me.* As soon as she wrote it, she knew it wasn't true. She picked up the telephone.

"Hullo!" Cissy was eating something, chewing.

"It's Sarah. I need a friend to talk to."

A muffled laugh. "That didn't take long. Come on over. Do you know the address and how to get here?"

"Yes." Sarah had figured it out a long time ago. Because she had known for months this day would come.

Cissy's house was very shabby-looking compared with the Shaheens'. It was in an old section of Tamarac, and the white paint was peeling and flaking over the door. The wrought-iron mailbox was crammed with envelopes and inserts, as if Cissy only cleaned it out every few days. A dog was barking somewhere, either the back of the house or the backyard. Sarah rang the bell.

The dog-barking escalated. Cissy answered the door in plaid shorts and a baggy green T-shirt. Scrubbed and dressed-down, she looked almost Sarah's age. "Come in, sweetheart." She held the screen open.

Sarah walked into a messy living room. This was a surprise, because Cissy was a marvelous professional housekeeper. Books and magazines were scattered on the floor. A pink towel covering one couch designated it as the one the dog used. The windowsills were crammed with little objects; tiny framed photos, candles, multicolored glass. A basket on the floor held an assortment of dog brushes, chewy sticks, and squeaky toys. Sarah had been hoping for witch balls and pentagrams.

"Do you live here by yourself?" Sarah heard herself ask, although she knew it was none of her business.

"Me and Caprice. Caprice is who you hear barking out in the yard. I put her out there because I didn't know if you liked dogs. Sometimes cat people don't like dogs."

"I like all animals," Sarah said. "You can let her in."

"Okay." Cissy grinned. "You asked for it."

She went somewhere in the back of the house, opened a door, and whistled. An Irish setter rocketed into the living room, bounding over Sarah, licking every square inch of exposed skin as Sarah squirmed and giggled.

"Down!" Cissy said, rushing to grab Caprice's collar. "Down. Mind your manners, Miss-miss. Sit. Good, sit. Down . . . good. Stay. Good girl, good, good girl." She knelt beside the dog and fondled her silky red ears. "You're the best girl ever. Did you know that?"

Caprice rolled on her back and pawed the air. Cissy patted her and looked up. "Want some tea?"

Sarah had kicked off her shoes and snuggled against a corner of the couch, watching Cissy play with the dog. An interesting feeling had been stealing over her. She felt cozy here. At home. Much more at home than she ever had with her real family. "Tea would be great."

While Cissy fussed in the kitchen, Sarah scanned the huge double bookcase in front of her. *Cosmos, Rocks and Minerals, Cross Creek, Your Florida Garden,* a set of detective novels by Dorothy Sayers, a set of novels by someone named Cherokee Paul McDonald. Several editions of the Bible. Interspersed with the books were pieces of driftwood and coral, pictures of the dog, and a little plaster lamb. On the wall over the dog's couch there was a huge framed watercolor of white tigers. While Sarah scanned these things, Caprice snuck over with a guilty expression and slowly climbed into the couch next to Sarah.

"You can sit with me," Sarah said, patting her. "I'd love to sit next to you."

Caprice flopped, bumping her hip heavily against Sarah's. Sarah stroked her thick, red coat and looked into her warm eyes. There was nothing in the world like communing with an animal. She missed it so much.

Cissy came in with a tray of tea and sandwiches. "Push her down if you don't want her there," she said, setting the tray on an end table and hauling the whole thing in front of Sarah's couch. "If you give that dog an inch, she'll take a mile."

"It's okay," Sarah said, petting Caprice. "She's a good doggy."

"Yes, she is." Cissy paused to smile at her dog. "Here. Help yourself."

There was a pot of some kind of wonderful-smelling tea, a plate of little tuna sandwiches garnished with watercress, and some small homemade cookies with pink icing. "I'm going to miss your cooking!" Sarah said.

Cissy poured them each a cup of tea. It was pale and fragrant. "I want you to come here anytime you want, Sarah," she said. "I'm real serious about that. You need at least one person to tell you you're not crazy, or you'll think you are. Believe me, I know."

Sarah sipped her tea. It tasted like flowers. She made a note to ask what it was. "Did you have someone to talk to when you first realized . . . you were psychic?"

Cissy blew a lock of hair out of her eyes and picked up a sandwich. She sat cross-legged on the couch. Her feet were bare. "No, I didn't. My mama was a Born-Again Christian. She drove my daddy to drink. Or his drinking drove her to be a Christian. Anyway when I started to have dreams—that's the way it started for me, with dreams—my mama took me straight to the minister, and you know what he blamed it on?" Cissy rolled her eyes.

"The devil?" Sarah shuddered a little.

"Don't you know it. He put his hand on my forehead and started screaming out this horrible prayer: 'Leave her! Leave her!' And when he was done, Mama took me home and gave me a good whipping with Daddy's belt to make sure that old demon was really uncomfortable. And after that, like you might imagine, I learned to keep my impressions to myself."

"God, you had it so much worse than I do. At least my parents are like rational, civilized people."

Cissy smiled wryly. "That could be worse, Sarah.

They don't believe in anything. The only explanation they have is something going haywire in your brain. I'd rather have a hundred whippings and a hundred exorcisms than one person giving me that look like I'm a nut."

Sarah chewed thoughtfully. "You're right."

"I learned to keep it to myself. Only talk to people who might understand. The worst thing in this world is to be different."

"I thought I could talk to Patrick," Sarah muttered. "But now I see I can't trust him at all."

"You can trust him. He's a good boy. He's just real scared right now. When you get scared, you don't take any chances with anything."

"Do you tell your boyfriends?" Sarah asked.

"Yeah, I tell them right off. And then I can tell by what they do if it's going to work out. If they don't ask any more about it, that's bad. If they start to tell me to go get help, that's bad. But a few of them think for a minute and ask me questions. Then I know they're all right. I haven't found anybody I would want to marry yet, but it isn't because I'm Talented. It's just other stuff."

"I'm asking because . . . you know I liked this boy Julian?"

"Yeah, I met him."

"While all this has been going on . . . at first I thought he was open-minded, but this morning I told him what happened last night and he started in on the same things my parents say, that I can't handle death and I need help and—"

"*He* can't handle death, honey. That's why you make

him nervous. But you shouldn't write him off. That's not what he wants. He's very drawn to you and you to him. You should never ignore feelings like that."

Sarah blinked. "I hadn't told you the part about breaking up with him yet."

"Yeah, well, being psychic saves time in conversation. Listen, this Julian is a nice boy. You aren't finished with him by a long shot."

As soon as Cissy said it, Sarah knew it was true. She was finished eating now and she sat back, arranging her feet comfortably around the dog, sipping slowly at her tea. "What do I do about this angry feeling I have for my family? I mean, it's great that you listen to me and you believe me, but I feel like none of them listened. I had something really . . . important to tell them, and none of them wanted to hear."

Cissy propped her feet on the other side of Caprice, who was snoring away. "You're a writer, aren't you?" she said. "You can always get the last word. You just remember everything that happened, Sarah. Don't forget any of the details. And when you grow up, you can write it, and nobody can stop you."

Sarah set her cup down. "You don't think writers like Stephen King and those guys are telling about things they think are real, do you?"

Cissy frowned. "*Real* is kind of a tricky word. And I'm not a writer, so I don't really know. But . . . I don't think they would want to write those kinds of things if they hadn't seen a few odd happenings in their time."

"My father—who won't admit this now—said that Irish people believe people are just a small part of a whole big universe full of invisible things."

Cissy nodded. "I think so too. The things I've seen . . . just seem like the edge of what might really be there."

"What should I be doing?" Sarah asked. "To develop this?"

Cissy shrugged. "It's more what you shouldn't do. Don't ignore your impressions. Don't fight your feelings or try to cut them off. And don't be afraid to risk feeling like a fool. That's the whole key to having miracles in your life, I think. You have to risk feeling like a fool."

Sarah smiled. "This is doing me a lot of good. What kind of tea is this, by the way?"

"Jasmine. Do you like it?"

"Yes! And it's weird. Jasmine is my favorite flower."

"I know."

Sarah smiled. "Did I ever tell you that?"

Cissy smiled back. "No."

Sixteen

Sarah slid open the heavy glass door and walked slowly to the middle of the sun porch. It was dawn. Lean shadows slashed the chartreuse lawn. The neighborhood was still.

The house behind her was also silent. Her father was already gone, and everyone else was a late riser. Sarah had always been the first one up, even as a little girl. But that was because Shadow would wake her.

She circled the porch twice, a slow trudge like a prisoner in an exercise yard, scanning for feelings. There was nothing there. Sarah sighed deeply, then yawned. She unlatched the screen and drifted into the yard.

The grass was drenched. Droplets of water collected on Sarah's sneakers, intact and glittering. She could smell privet and bahia grass and cypress. Not jasmine. She made a mental note to write in her blank book that certain smells were more active at certain times of day.

Sarah paused at the hibiscus hedge. She plucked a

handful of wet blossoms, knelt, and placed them on the grave. Almost immediately a breeze stirred and scattered them. Sarah felt rejected. She sat in the wet grass, feeling the dew soak into her shorts. Her throat tightened. She covered her face with both hands and cried.

When she looked up, the angle of light had shifted. The grass was dryer. There was traffic in the streets. A dog barked somewhere. Sarah wiped her eyes and pulled her knees up. She could feel as lonely and bereft as she wanted to, but the world was going to go right on.

She heard footsteps behind her in the grass. She knew it was Patrick, without looking around. She wondered if she knew the footsteps of everyone in the family, or if she was being psychic, or if it was just an educated guess, since anyone else would call from the house, not walk out to her.

She wondered if she should start being nice to him again. They hadn't spoken since yesterday morning, when he had betrayed her.

He didn't speak. He simply sat down in the grass beside her. He cradled a cup of coffee in both hands. He frowned at Shadow's grave. He might have been out there by himself. Sarah decided she wouldn't speak to him at all unless he offered a sincere and humiliating apology. That was something he was good at anyway.

Patrick looked at Sarah. Sarah looked away, then back at him. He held out the coffee cup and made an interrogatory noise. Sarah shook her head. He took a swig and set the cup in the grass. The liquid inside tilted dangerously. "Brian's dropping out of school," he said.

Sarah was torn. If she held out for an apology, she

wouldn't get to discuss this interesting topic. She picked up the coffee cup and took a drink. "For good?"

Patrick held out his hands for the cup, and Sarah passed it to him. He sipped and passed it back to her. He was clever. "For the entire foreseeable future. He blames a lot of·this on the pressure he was under to perform. He's not a scholar like me or a raw genius like you. He was just trying to make Dad's master plan work. I feel sorry for him really. Dad always wants everyone to be something they're not."

There was a personal confession in that, but Sarah decided to let it pass for now. "You and Brian seem to be getting pretty chummy here," she said. "Did you bond when you were trying to murder each other?"

He cleared his throat. "We scared the shit out of ourselves when we were trying to murder each other. Brian was . . . he came to me yesterday—don't say I told you this—but he was *crying*."

"Our Brian?"

"Our Brian. I hardly said a word. He made a speech like Gandhi, about how we've got to stop all this and learn to get along. He told me all these reasons he's jealous of me. I couldn't believe it. Him jealous of me. I mean, that's funny. Anyway he wants to get his own place here in town and get a job. God knows what he thinks he could do, but at least it's better than him pretending he's going to be a doctor when he can't add two and two."

Sarah smiled a little. "Maybe Mom could get him a job at the paper."

Patrick chuckled. He offered Sarah the last sip of coffee.

She tilted her head back to drink. The sun splayed like a halo through the branches of the palm trees. "What about Karen?"

"Karen?"

"You know, the naked girl who smashed our coffee table."

"Oh, Karen. Oh, well, she's either Brian's or she's nobody's. I never liked her. You knew that. You hit me over the head with it constantly."

"So you just went along with her plan to hurt Brian because that was your plan too?"

"What is this, Confession? It was partly that, but also I guess I wanted to see what Brian's life was like. I'll never go out with a babe like that. And, you know, while it was going on, Dad was showing me a lot of respect."

"You guys are both so dumb. Dad wants one son who's an A-student and another one who's a lady-killer. There's a role for each of you there if you'd just be smart and pick the right one."

"Yeah, but if I was as wise as you, Sarah, I'd have to be obnoxious like you are."

She laughed and swatted at him. "I went to Cissy's yesterday."

"Is that where you went?"

"Yes. I might go there a lot. She's a friend."

"She's a special person."

Sarah looked at him sideways. "You think so?"

He looked away. "Sure."

"She likes you too."

"How do you know? She never said that."

"I'm psychic, remember?"

Patrick hugged his knees. "Well, she knows my number. I'm in the book."

"You are dumb. All you have to do is drive me over there when I go to visit."

A little smile broke over his face. "Oh, yeah! But, jeez, if something . . . I mean, it won't, but if something miraculous happened and she and I started dating, it would be so awkward for Mom. She'd have to be nice to someone she fired. . . . God! this is the perfect plan!"

Sarah laughed. "Listen, now that your life is all worked out, you're in big trouble with me."

He nodded. "I know."

"Did you or did you not see that cat in the kitchen?"

"Sarah, everything was so crazy. I mean, I was being killed and all. Do I have to—"

"Yes, you do. You made me look and feel like I was crazy in front of the whole family. Did you see Shadow?"

He sighed deeply. "I sure as fuck saw something."

"And *something* attacked Brian and made him let go of you? And *something* accidentally put a scratch on your chest?"

"Yeah, I guess so. Sarah, this stuff scares me."

"How would you feel if you were me? I've known she was here all summer."

"I know. I've been thinking about your dreams and all."

The sun was high in the sky now. The yard was growing uncomfortably hot. In a minute they'd have to go inside. She looked at the grave one more time. Except for the marker it looked like any other part of the garden. Shadow was really and truly gone.

"I'm going to have a weird life," Sarah said.

Patrick slapped her arm gently. "Join the club, Sis."

Sarah picked up the phone three times, and three times she put it back down. On the fourth try she managed to dial Julian's number. He answered on the first ring.

"Hello?"

"Hi."

"Oh, hi!" He sounded happy.

"Have you thought about what I said?"

"Yes. Have you thought about what I said?"

"Yes. And I think we need to talk some more."

"Great! I mean, I think so too. You know, Sarah, this is a big question. With lots of sides to it. It might take us a long time to talk it out completely. Years even."

Sarah laughed. "Yeah. Years."

Sarah wondered which of her parents would come to talk to her about her sanity. She knew they would discuss it and assign one of them the job. She wasn't surprised that evening when her father got another doctor to take his calls and asked if she'd like to go out with him for ice cream, just the two of them. It was a logical choice. He had the medical background, so he could evaluate her sense of reality. Plus he was a diplomat. They probably figured he could sneak up on her better than Mrs. Shaheen.

They drove to a Dairy Queen in Coral Springs. Sarah had to place the order because Dr. Shaheen always got flustered and confused by fast-food menus and counter service. He was always asking for a Whopper at McDonald's and that kind of thing.

Sarah chose a Blizzard for her father and a Peanut Buster Parfait for herself. For a while they sat in the car, spooning in silence, watching twilight fall. Sarah decided to be quiet and just react to what he said.

"Pretty scary stuff the other night," he said finally.

Sarah laughed. "You're telling me."

"It must be upsetting," he said, "to see your own brothers go at it that way."

She dug for peanuts in the bottom of the plastic glass. They never put enough peanuts in the thing. Sarah liked to come out with each bite containing a little ice cream, a little fudge, and one peanut. "Sure," she said. "But I've seen them fight before."

"I know, but not like this. And you were having an upsetting summer anyway. I mean, I know you're not over—" He gestured with his spoon.

"Shadow's death. At least I can say it."

He laughed. "Touché. What is this thing again? Is it supposed to have these green specks in it?"

"Yes, Daddy. It's got M&M's inside it, ground up in little pieces."

"The M&M's people agree to that?"

She giggled. "I guess so. Anyway I am over it. Well, at least I can accept it. She came back to help Patrick in the fight, but now she's gone. Nothing I do can bring her back."

He frowned, apparently having trouble with his diagnosis. "Your mother says Cissy put a lot of wild ideas in your head."

Sarah looked at him very seriously. "They were already there. She just made me feel like they were okay."

"Well, maybe they are. Something kind of astonishing happened to me this morning."

Sarah looked up. "What?"

"Patrick came to see me at the hospital. He virtually made an appointment to see me. He corroborated the whole cat business. Said he and Brian both saw some kind of cat thing jump into the middle of the fight. Just as you said. Now, that either means something strange really did happen or Patrick is very loyal and wants to protect you."

"It's both, Daddy. Brian saw the cat too. He said so. It's just that . . . you know, it's scary to say things to people that sound crazy. How many people did you tell when you saw your grandfather's ghost?"

"Everyone I told thought it was a product of grief."

"Is that what you think?"

He stuck his spoon in the ice cream. "Who's interviewing whom?"

"Tell me. Do you think you saw a real ghost?"

"That's certainly the way I experienced it."

"And did that bother you or make you weird? Was it anything anybody needed to worry about?"

"I get your point, honey. But . . . a lot has happened, and your mother and I *are* worried about you."

"Dad, I'll probably always have these kinds of things happening to me. It's part of who I am, just like it is with Cissy. She's the most rational person I've ever known. If

I think you guys are going to worry, I'll just stop telling you about it."

He spooned up his Blizzard thoughtfully.

"Stop telling your mother," he said finally.

Sarah smiled down into her ice cream.

"I saw a patient today whose cat just had kittens."

"Daddy!"

"I'm just telling you. They need a good home. What's wrong with starting over? Anyway I told her we'd come over in a few weeks when they're ready for adoption and you'd take a look at them."

"Daddy, Shadow was special. I'll never have another cat like her again."

"So? Does that mean you can't ever have another cat?"

Sarah sighed. "This is your price for getting Mom off my back, isn't it?"

"Uh, yeah. It is. Take it or leave it."

Sarah searched the sludge at the bottom of her glass for a final nut. No such luck. "I guess nobody ever died from looking at a bunch of stupid kittens."

The patient turned out to be a divorced woman named Toni Fairbanks. She had a condo in Lauderhill. Sarah's father seemed to know the way without consulting any directions. He seemed to know right where the guest parking area was, too, without any fumbling around. On behalf of her mother, Sarah made the decision to be as frosty as possible to Toni Fairbanks and possibly to her kittens as well.

The front door was opened by a tall, shapely woman in white tennis shorts. She had blond, flyaway hair, brown eyes, and freckles across her nose. She was wearing pale-pink lipstick, like from the sixties. "Hi, Bill!" She smiled warmly. "This must be Sarah."

"How do you do," Sarah said, glaring at her.

"Come on in," said Toni Fairbanks, leading them into a cool, shadowy hallway with black-slate tiles. Watching the back of her shorts, Sarah didn't think she walked like a very nice lady. "How about some iced tea and cookies?" she said over her shoulder. "Then I'll have Lydia get the kitties out."

"Lydia is Toni's little girl," Sarah's father explained. He was keeping his eyes on the shorts too.

They were led into a messy living room strewn with the brilliant pinks and purples of little girls' toys. Mermaids and unicorns were everywhere, along with a few oddities Sarah didn't understand. For instance on the coffee table there was a doll with pink hair who seemed to be rising out of a giant cupcake.

"Just clear some junk and have a seat," said Toni Fairbanks. She always seemed to be talking over her shoulder. She disappeared into what must have been the kitchen and began making ice-cube sounds.

Sarah's father perched on the edge of a chair. He looked guilty.

"What's her problem?" Sarah asked him.

He jumped a bit. "What?"

Sarah smiled sweetly. "What did you treat her for?"

"Oh, strep throat. She's prone to colds."

"Maybe she should wear more clothes."

Before he could respond to that, a little girl, presum-

ably Lydia, appeared in the doorway. She wore brilliant-
blue stirrup pants and some kind of long T-shirt with a
picture of a chubby cat on it. The shirt said HAPPY HAPPY
JOY JOY. Sarah began to feel old, not knowing the cartoon
characters anymore. Lydia looked nothing like her
mother, had a mass of jet-black hair that framed her
face, and stuck out slightly all around, like a broom. She
leaned on the doorframe, pulling up one foot like a stork
and holding it in both hands. "Hi," she said shyly.

"Hi, Lydia," said Dr. Shaheen. "Remember me?"

"Sure," she said. "Did you come for the kitty?"

"Yes," he said. "This is my daughter, Sarah, and she
loves kitties."

Lydia came into the room and stopped squarely in
front of Sarah. Up close she did resemble her mother.
Her face was pale and freckled. Her eyes, under black
lashes, were a deep brown. "Are you his little girl?" she
asked.

"That's right." Sarah smiled.

"I'm Mommy's little girl. Mommy's in the kitchen."

"Yeah," Sarah said. "Getting cookies. Who's that on
your shirt?"

Lydia took a handful of shirt in each fist and held it
out like a tent flap. "Stimpy."

"Oh," said Sarah. "Of course. I see now. How many
kitties do you have?"

Lydia dropped the shirt and hoisted herself onto the
coffee table. "We have Wanda, who is our cat for always.
We aren't going to get rid of her." She shook her head
no for emphasis. "Wanda is a white cat with blue eyes
and she can't hear anything."

"She's deaf?" Sarah said.

"No, she's alive. But she had five kittens." A splayed hand was presented, then each finger was carefully grabbed in sequence. "One is all black with a star. Two is black and white like a pony. Three is like two, but with more black on him. Four is black with white booties on. And five is white like Wanda."

Sarah mentally chose the blackest one. It would be something like Shadow anyway. "Do they have names?"

"No. We're going to give them to good homes, and those people can name them."

"I see."

Toni returned with a tray of iced tea and Oreos. "Do you want to go and look at the kittens right away, Sarah? We'll save a glass of iced tea for you."

Sarah didn't especially want to see her father interact with this woman. "I don't even think I'm thirsty. Lydia can show me the cats."

"Lydia, take Sarah back to your room and show her the kitties."

"Okay." Lydia hopped down, loaded one fist with cookies, and extended the other hand to Sarah. "Come on!"

Sarah let herself be dragged down a shadowy hallway into a little room that looked like a pastel tornado had hit it. "I never saw so many toys," she said.

Lydia didn't reply. She was in her closet, dragging out a cardboard box full of mewling kittens. As she did so, a large white cat followed, sniffing and looking concerned.

"That's Wanda," Lydia said. "And these are the babies." As soon as she stopped dragging the box, the five kittens jumped out and fanned out over the room, exploring and sniffing. Their mother watched them fretfully, shooting nervous glances at Sarah.

Sarah looked first to the almost-all-black kitten. It was gnawing on the edge of a plastic truck. It had big feet like a rabbit and a rather stupid look on its face. Sarah decided not to be too hasty. She sat on the edge of Lydia's unmade bed. "Do you know which ones are girls?" she asked.

"Yes," Lydia said. "That one," she pointed to the rear end of the pony-spotted cat, who was struggling to burrow into a small tennis shoe. "And that one." She pointed to the all-white, who was not hopping around and exploring like the others. She had climbed out of the box and sat on the floor. She was staring at Sarah.

"Is that one—" Sarah almost said "deaf" again. "Can that white one hear, or is she like her mother?"

"White cats can't hear anything," Lydia said. "Look." She went over to the white kitten and said loudly, "Hey!" The other four kittens all jumped. The mother cat and the white kitten sat serenely.

"If you have a kitty like Wanda who can't hear, you have to take extra good care of them and keep them safe," Lydia commented.

"Yes, I can imagine," Sarah said. The white kitten, still holding Sarah's gaze, took a few steps toward her and sat down again. The gaze was disarming in its intensity. Familiar. "When were these kittens born?" Sarah asked. "It was about six weeks ago, wasn't it?"

"I don't know. They're six weeks old, though. That's when you can let people adopt them because they don't need their Mommy anymore."

Maybe any deaf cat would stare at a stranger like

that, though. After all, she was defenseless. But the mother cat was busy doing something else, trying to pick up the kitten with its head in the tennis shoe. She wasn't staring. Sarah looked into the white kitten's eyes. She knew that cat. She knew that cat as surely as she knew Patrick or Brian or anyone. Sarah carefully enunciated the words in her mind. *Shadow? Is that you?*

The kitten immediately came forward, walking right to Sarah's feet and sitting down again, staring up into her face.

I am cracking up, Sarah thought. *This is the craziest thing I've ever come up with.* She leaned down and picked the kitten up. It made no protest, settling comfortably in Sarah's arms.

"She likes you," Lydia commented.

Sarah wasn't listening. She was thinking about Cissy and everything she'd said about magic being possible if people would only take the risk and let it happen. On Lydia's wall there was a poster of a mouse wearing a tall magician's hat with the moon and stars. It said BELIEVE AND MAKE IT SO.

"Did you make up your mind?" Lydia asked. "Is that your kitty?"

Sarah looked down at the bright blue eyes that gazed up at her with absolute trust. Her own eyes began to burn with tears. "Yes," she said. "This is my kitty."